LITTLE PIERROT

 **1** Get the Moon

CUB
HOUSE

J-GN
LITTLE PIERROT
458-7500

Publisher's Cataloging-In-Publication Data

(Prepared by The Donohue Group, Inc.)

Names: Varanda, Alberto, author, illustrator. | Melloul, Jeremy, translator.

Title: Little Pierrot. 1, Get the moon / Alberto Varanda ; [translation by Jeremy Melloul].

Other Titles: Petit Pierrot. [Volume 1], Décrocher la Lune. English | Get the moon

Description: [St. Louis, Missouri] : The Lion Forge, LLC, 2017. | Translation of: Petit Pierrot. [Volume 1], Décrocher la Lune. Toulon : Editions Soleil, ©2010. | Summary: "Little Pierrot is a young boy with a very large imagination and his head forever in the stars. Joined by his snail buddy, the aptly named Mr. Snail, he sets off to explore the boundaries of space in a series of magical and surreal adventures: first to reach the Moon, and then the Stars."--Provided by publisher.

Identifiers: ISBN 978-1-941302-59-0

Subjects: LCSH: Boys--Comic books, strips, etc. | Imagination--Comic books, strips, etc. | Snails--Comic books, strips, etc. | Outer space--Exploration--Comic books, strips, etc. | CYAC: Boys--Cartoons and comics. | Imagination--Cartoons and comics. | Snails--Cartoons and comics. | Outer space--Exploration--Cartoons and comics. | LCGFT: Graphic novels.

Classification: LCC PN6747.V37 P4813 2017 | DDC 741.5944 [Fic]--dc23

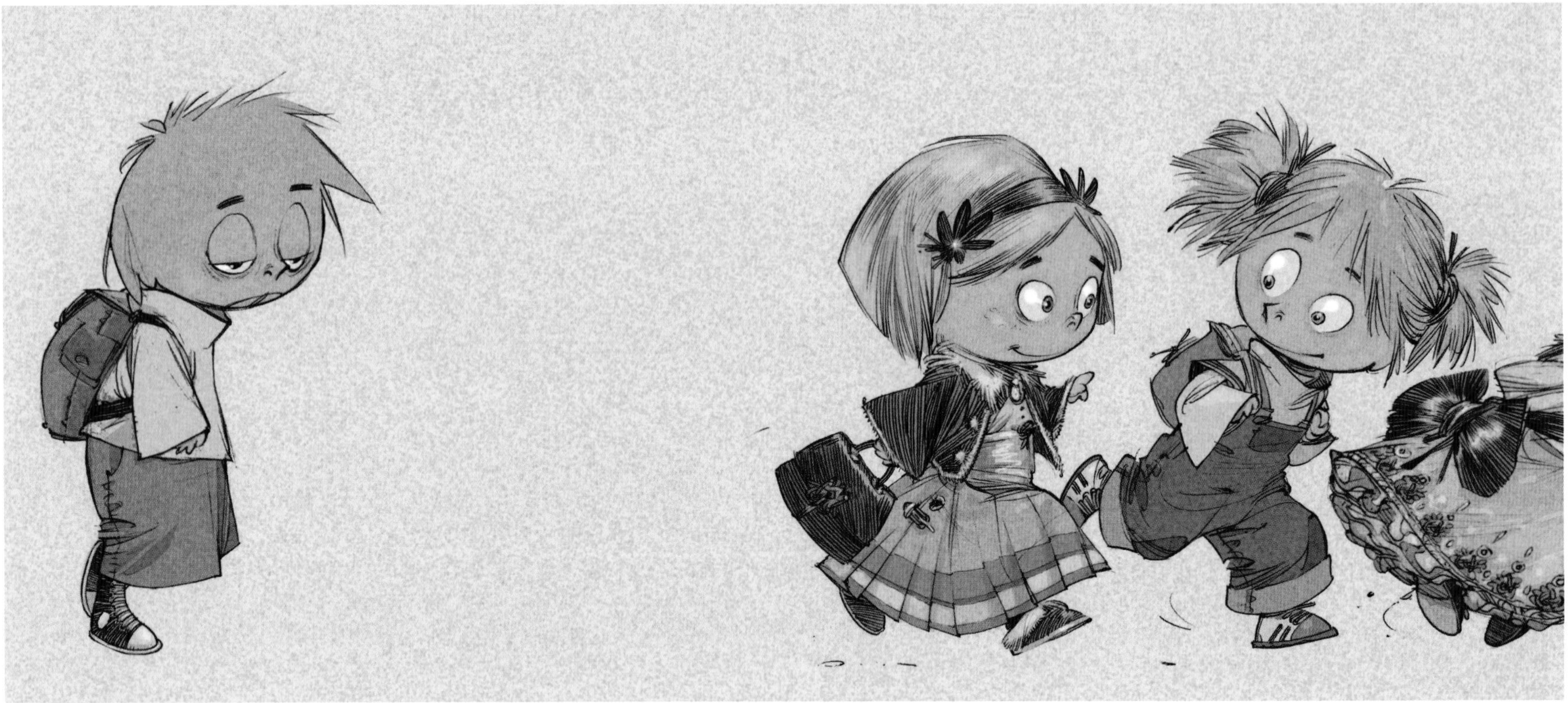

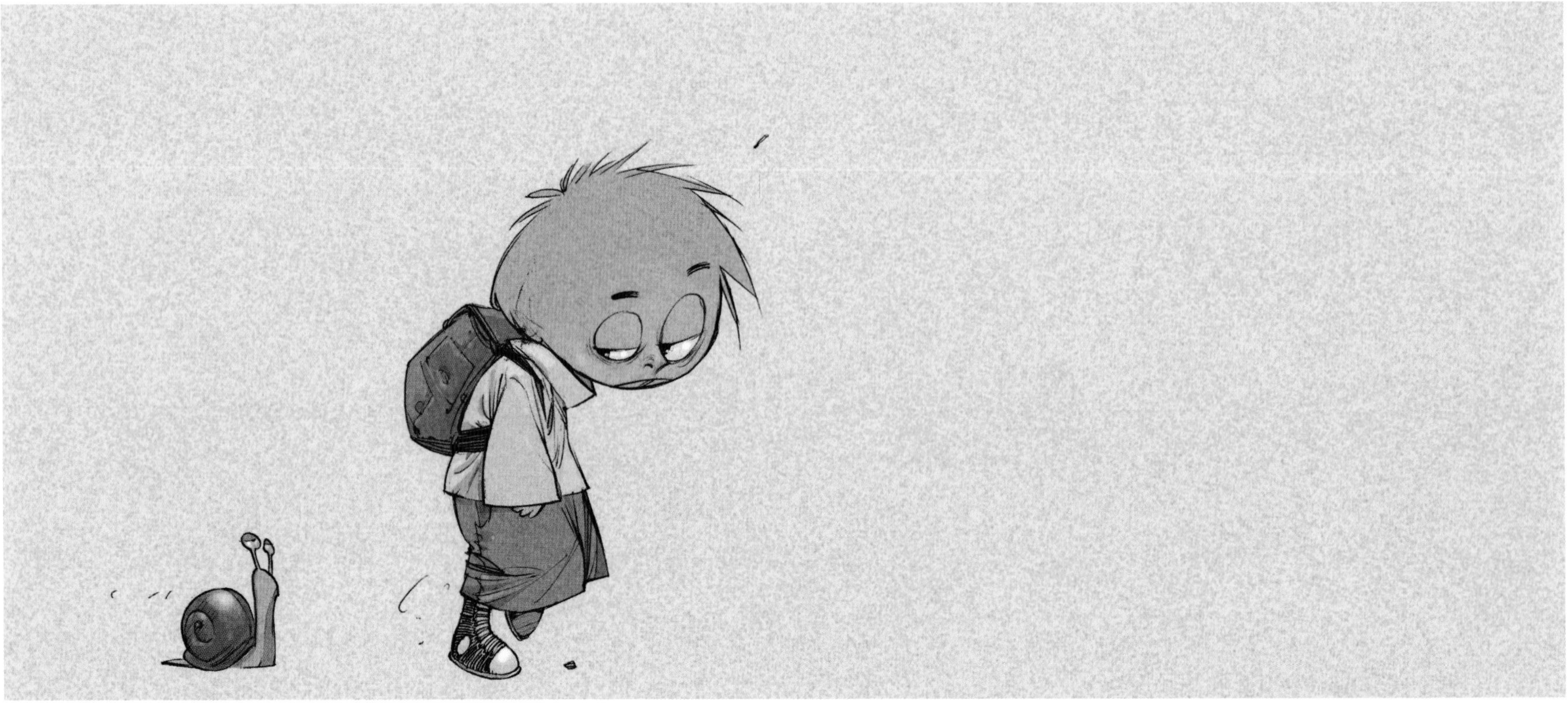

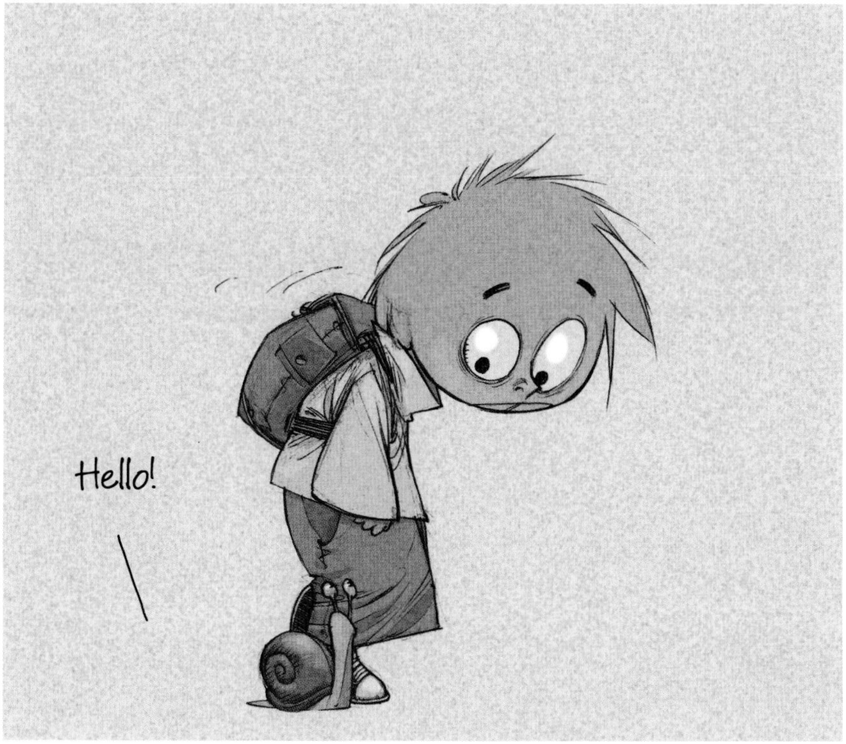
Hello!

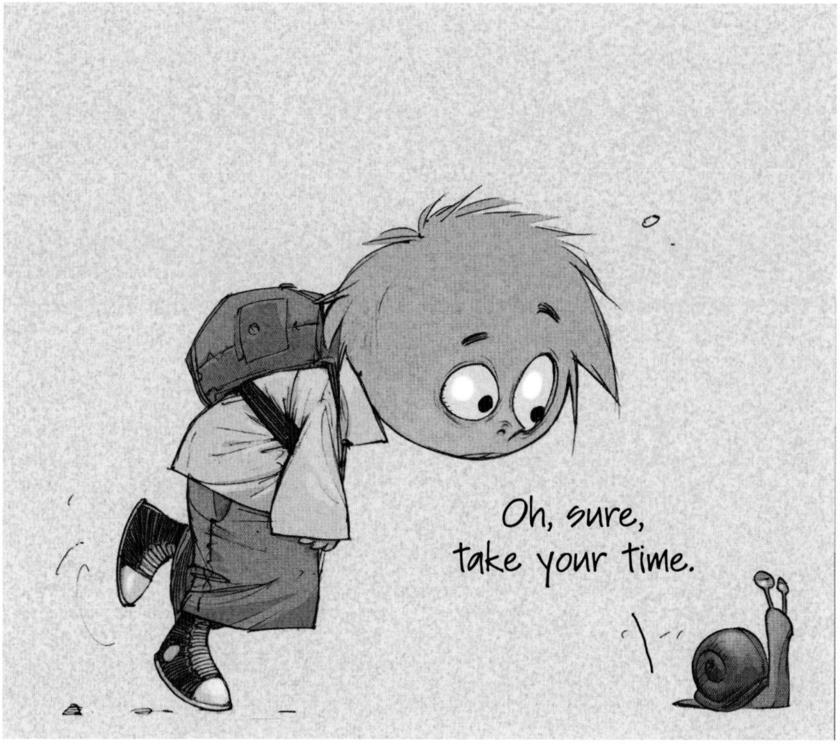
Oh, sure, take your time.

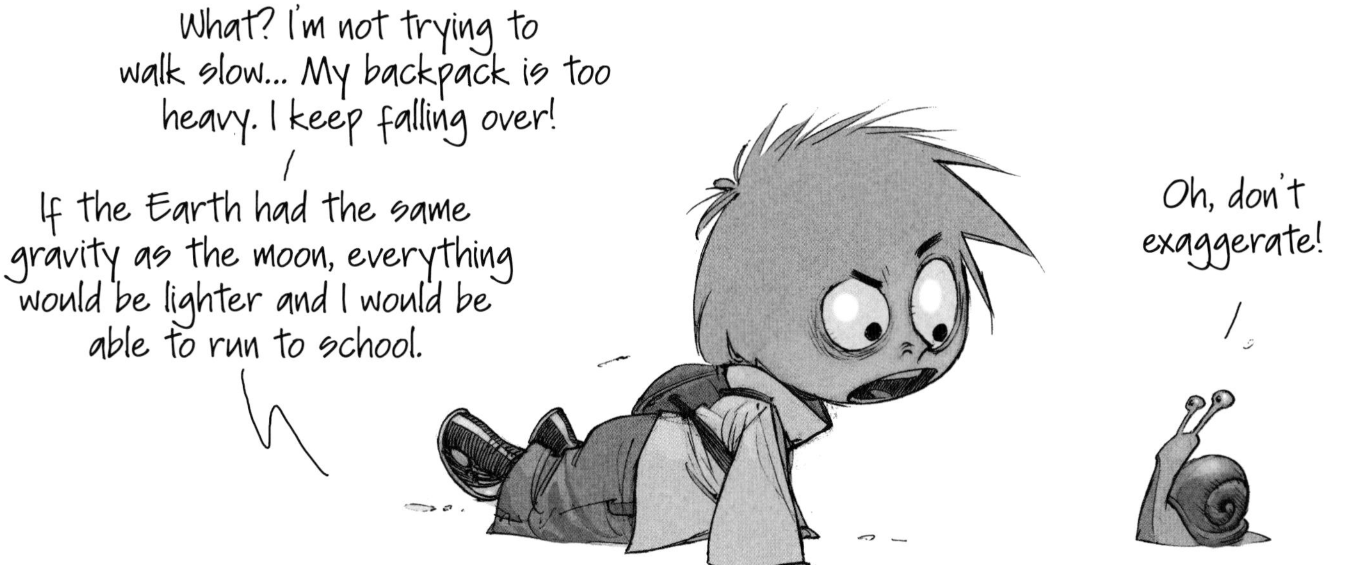
What? I'm not trying to walk slow... My backpack is too heavy. I keep falling over!
If the Earth had the same gravity as the moon, everything would be lighter and I would be able to run to school.
Oh, don't exaggerate!

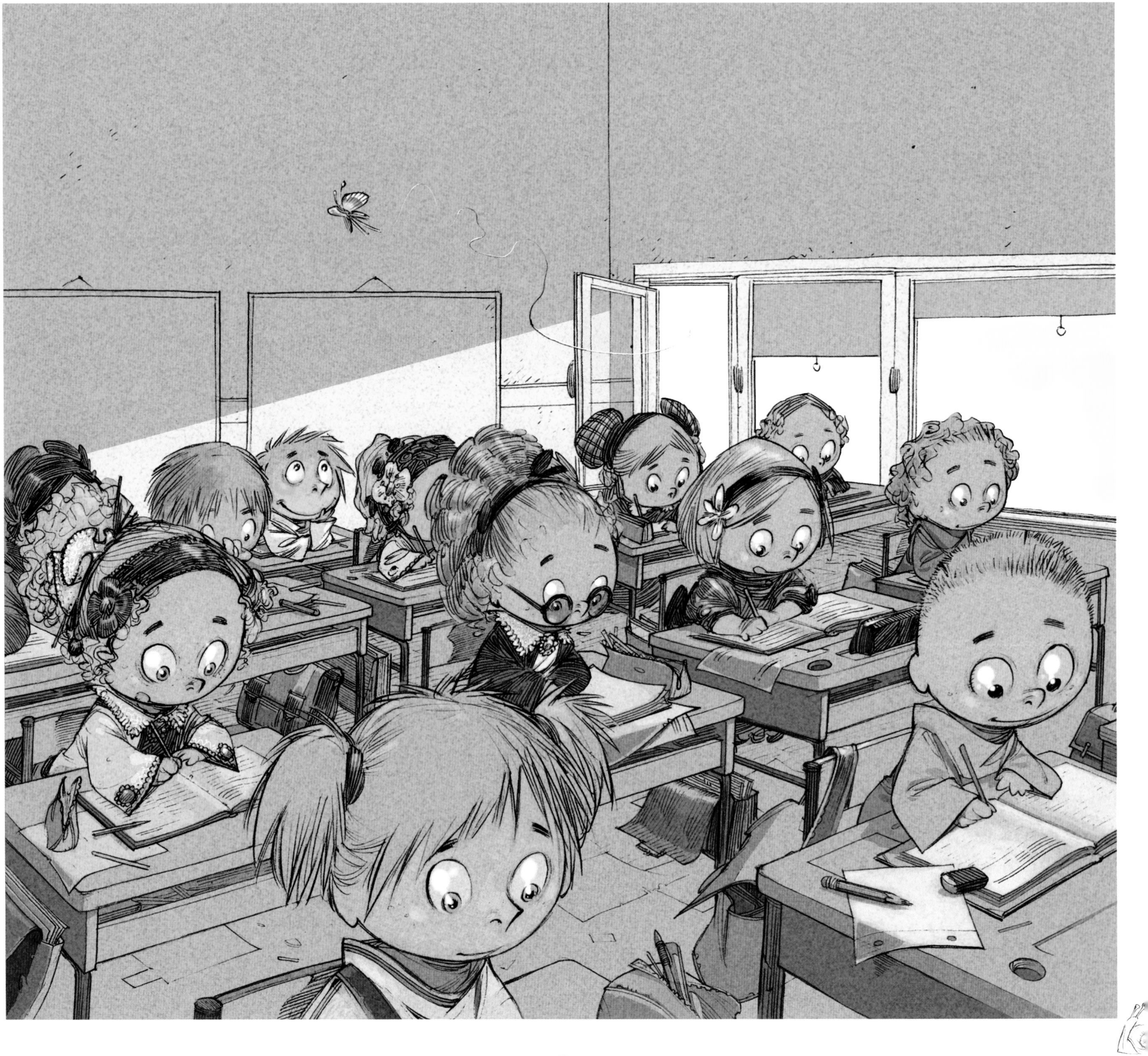

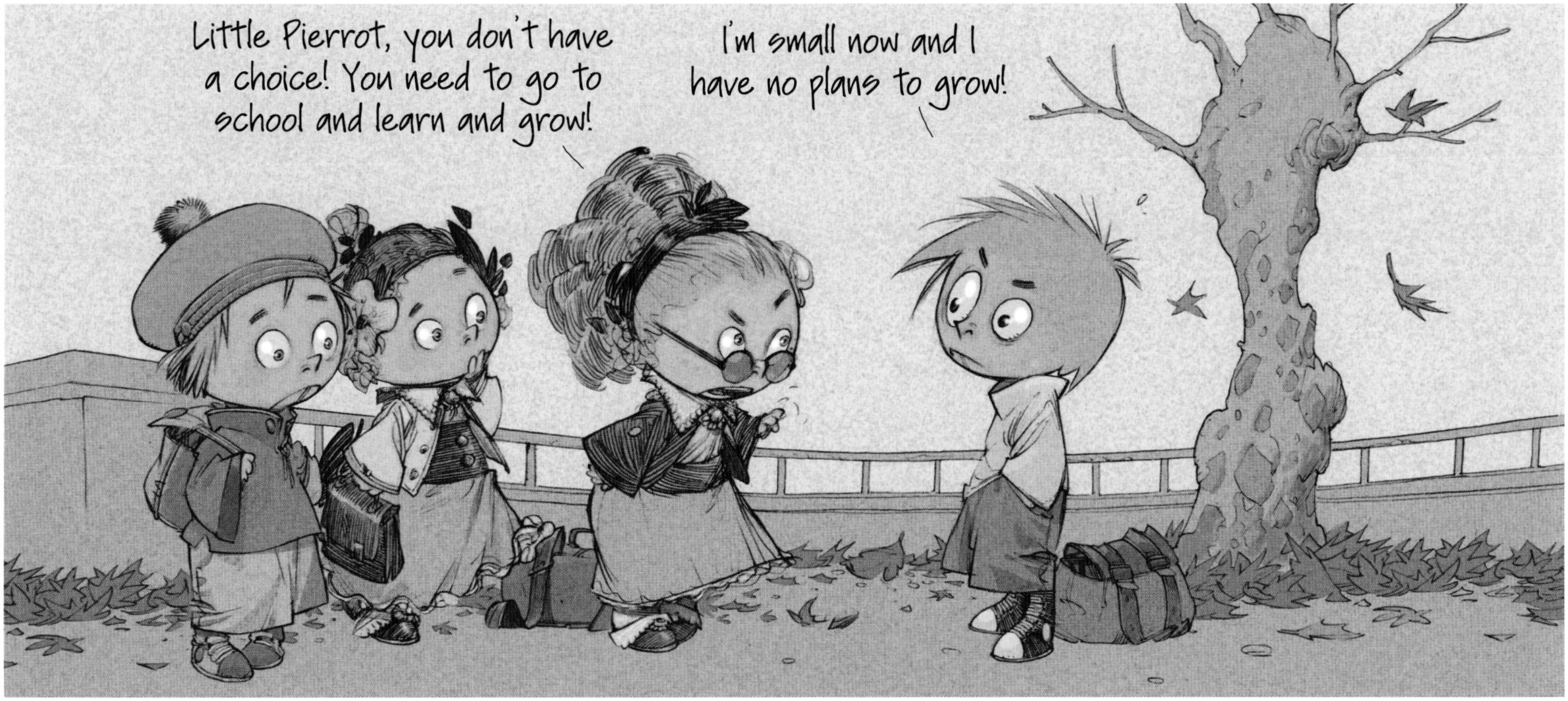
Little Pierrot, you don't have a choice! You need to go to school and learn and grow!
I'm small now and I have no plans to grow!

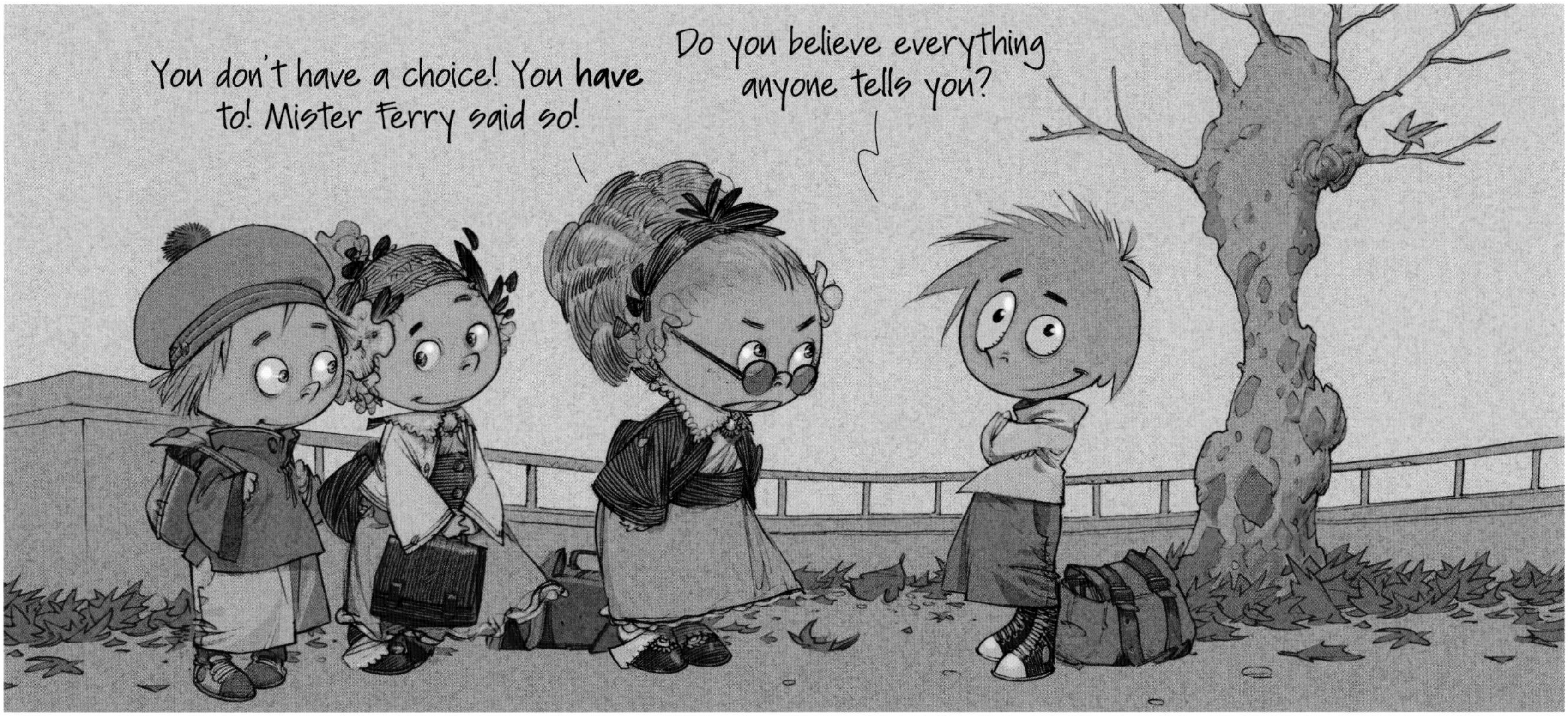
You don't have a choice! You **have** to! Mister Ferry said so!
Do you believe everything anyone tells you?

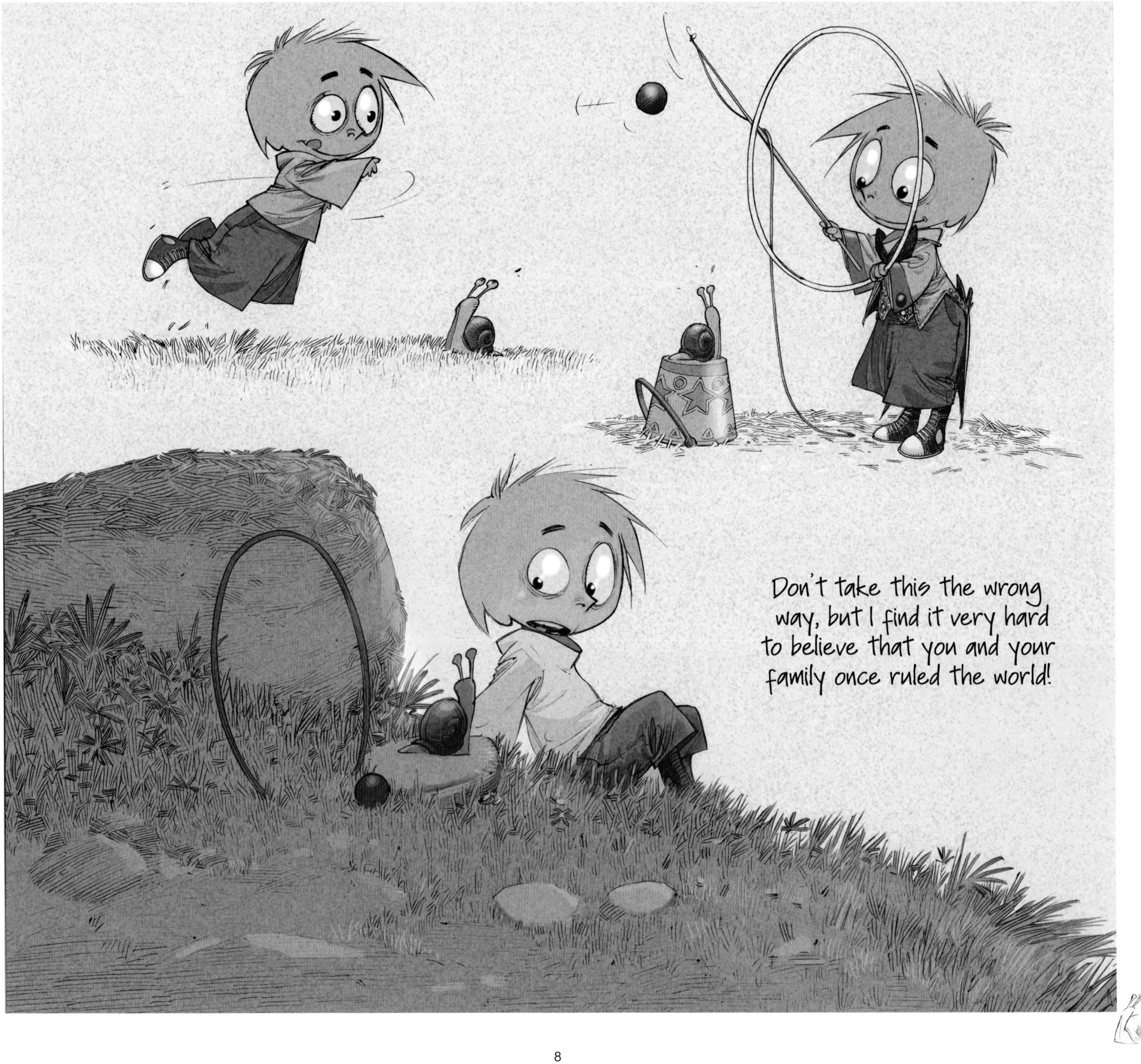

Don't take this the wrong way, but I find it very hard to believe that you and your family once ruled the world!

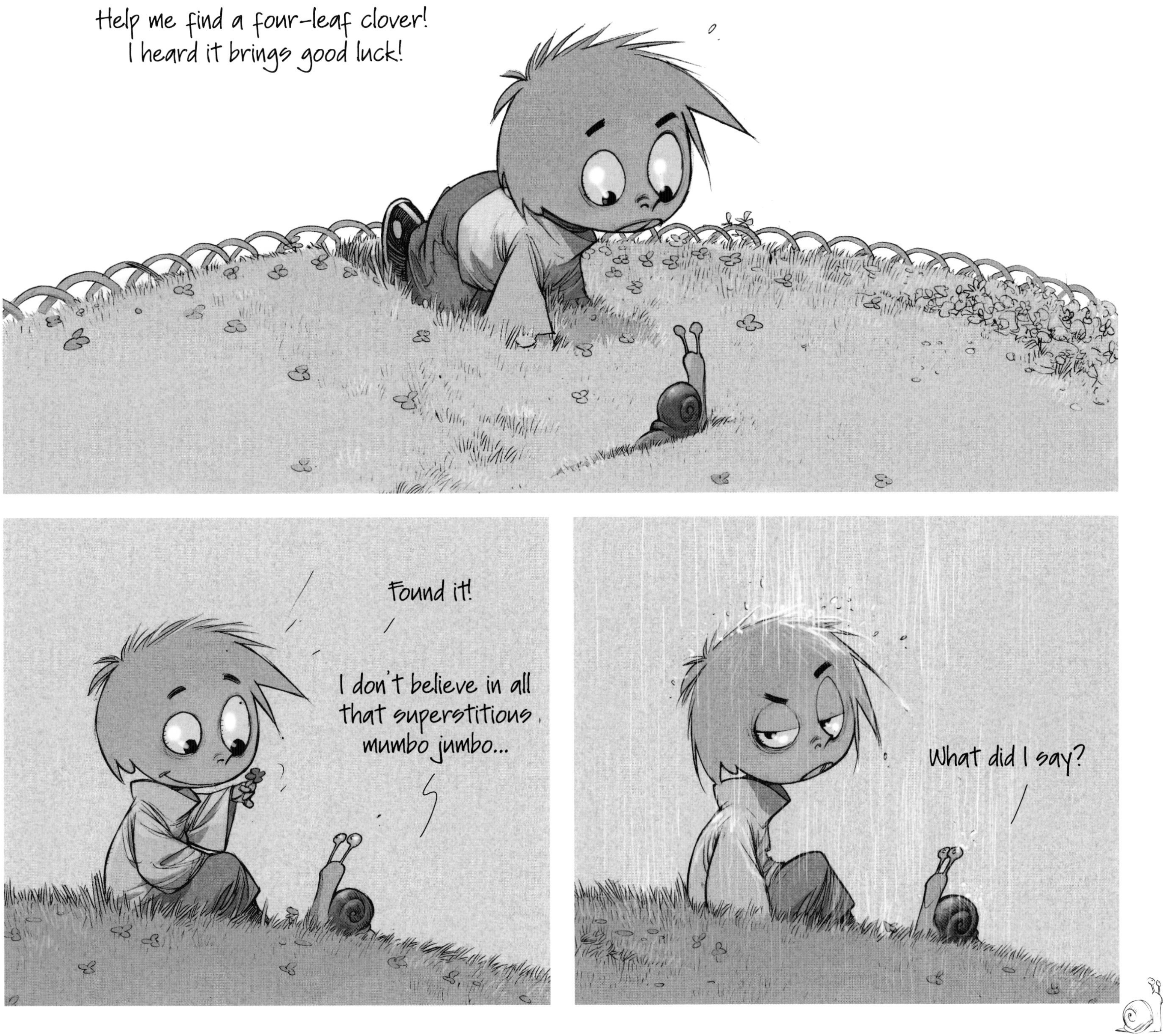
Help me find a four-leaf clover!
I heard it brings good luck!
Found it!
I don't believe in all that superstitious mumbo jumbo...
What did I say?

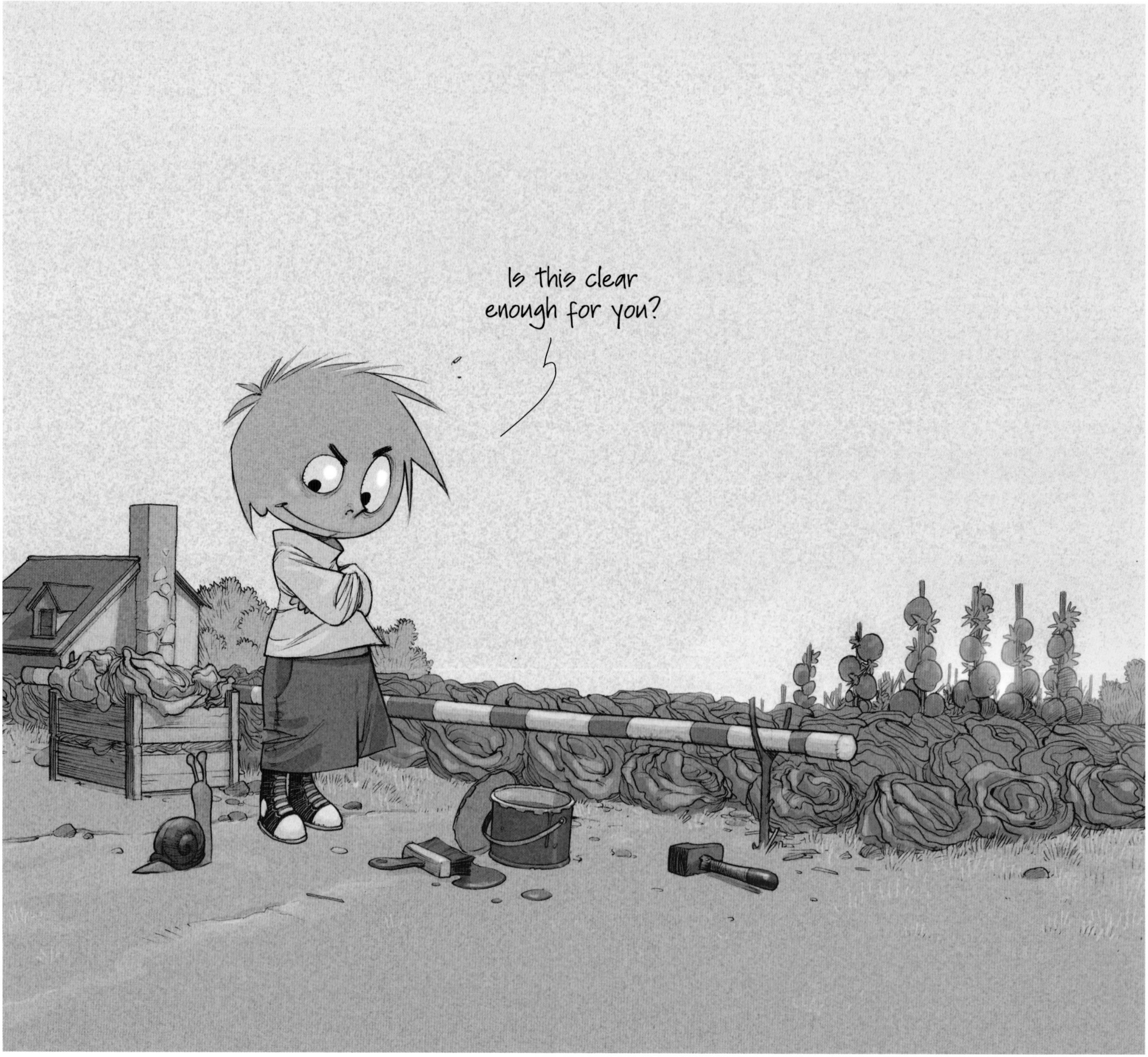
Is this clear
enough for you?

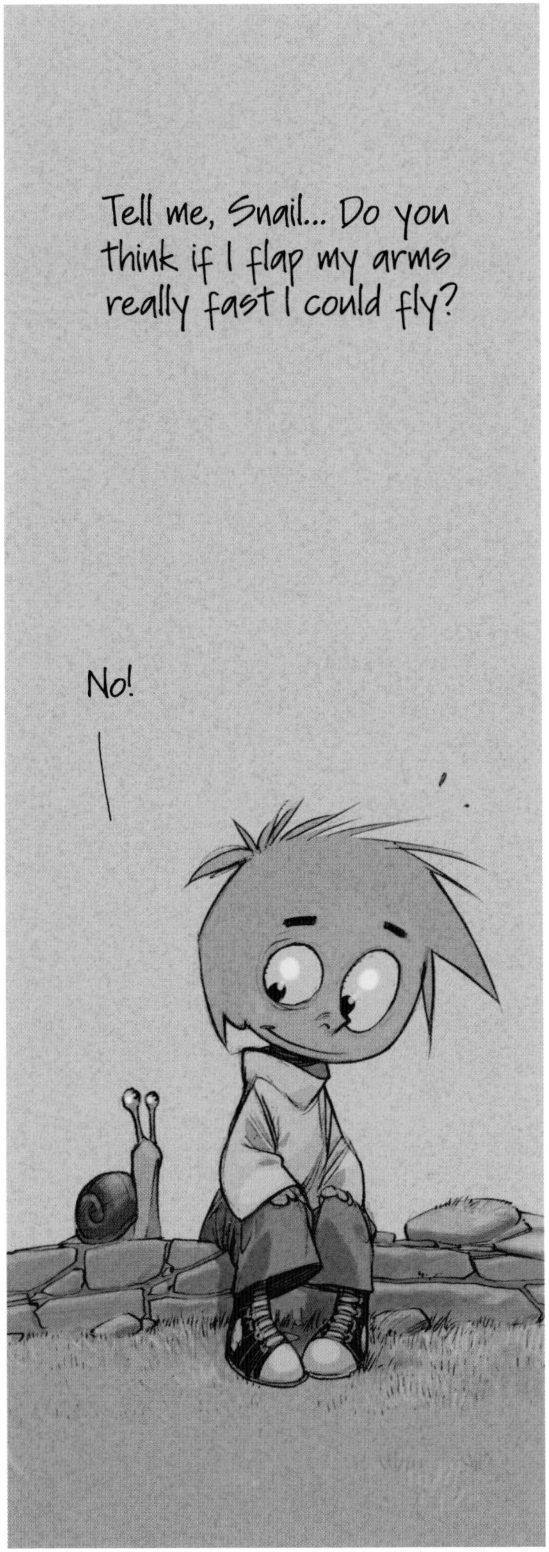
Tell me, Snail... Do you think if I flap my arms really fast I could fly?
No!

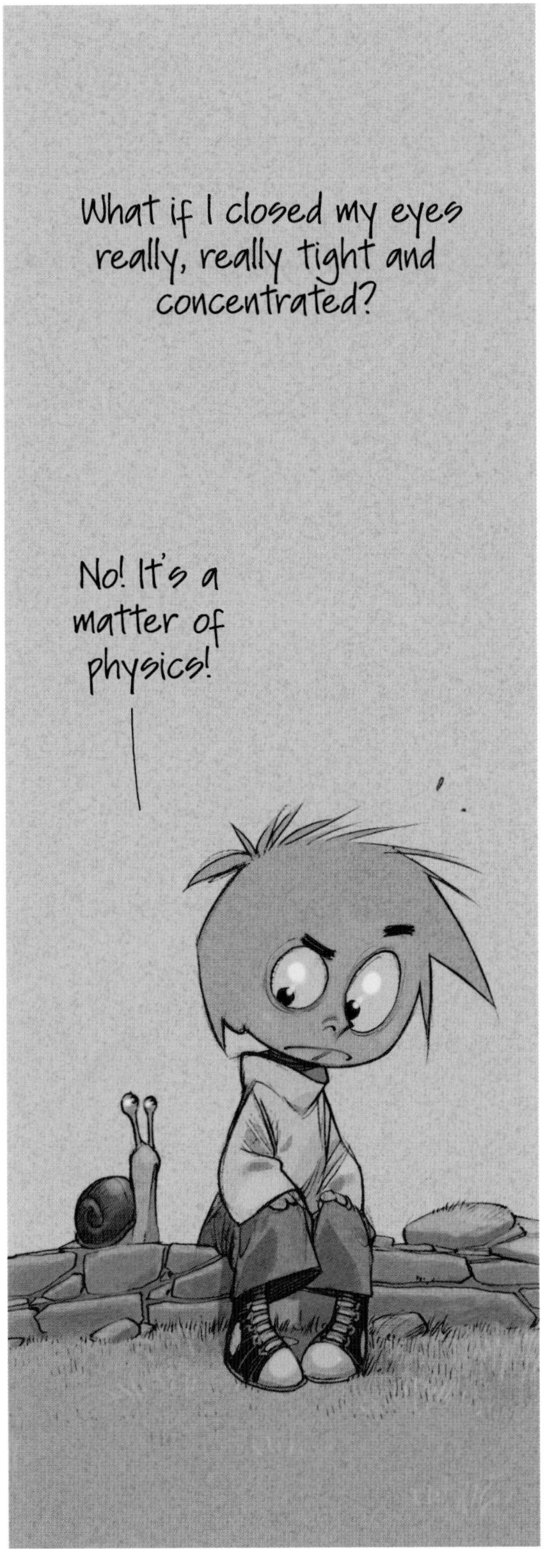
What if I closed my eyes really, really tight and concentrated?
No! It's a matter of physics!

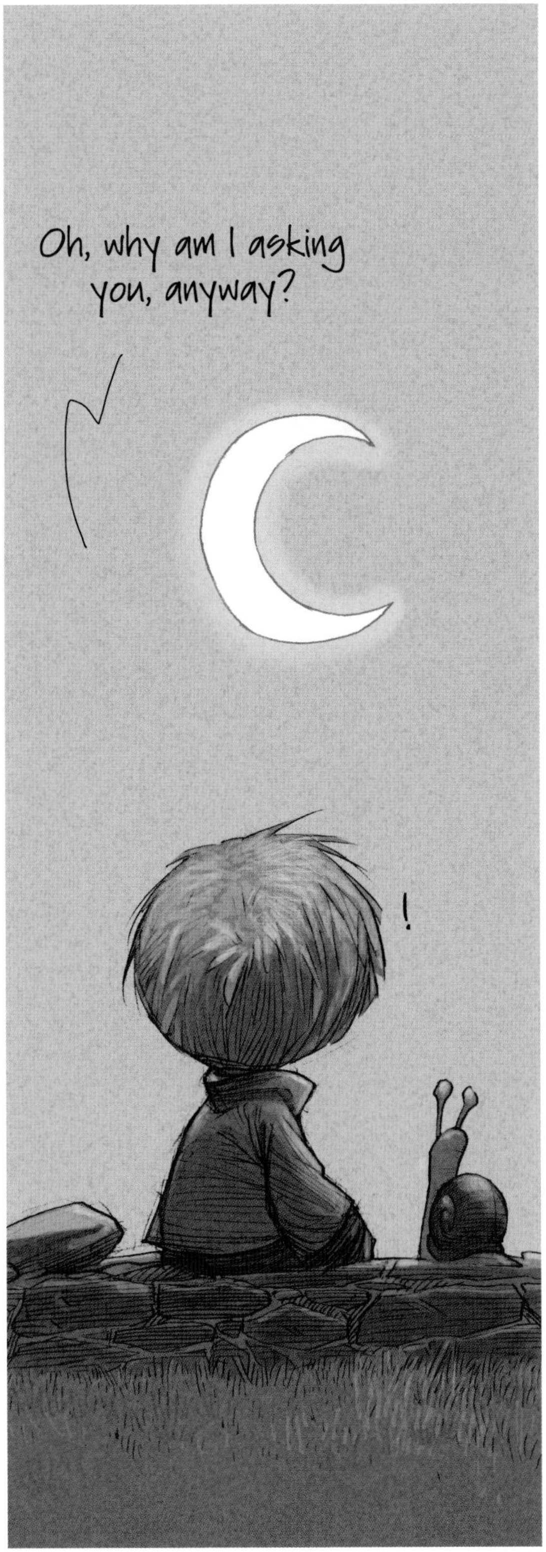
Oh, why am I asking you, anyway?
!

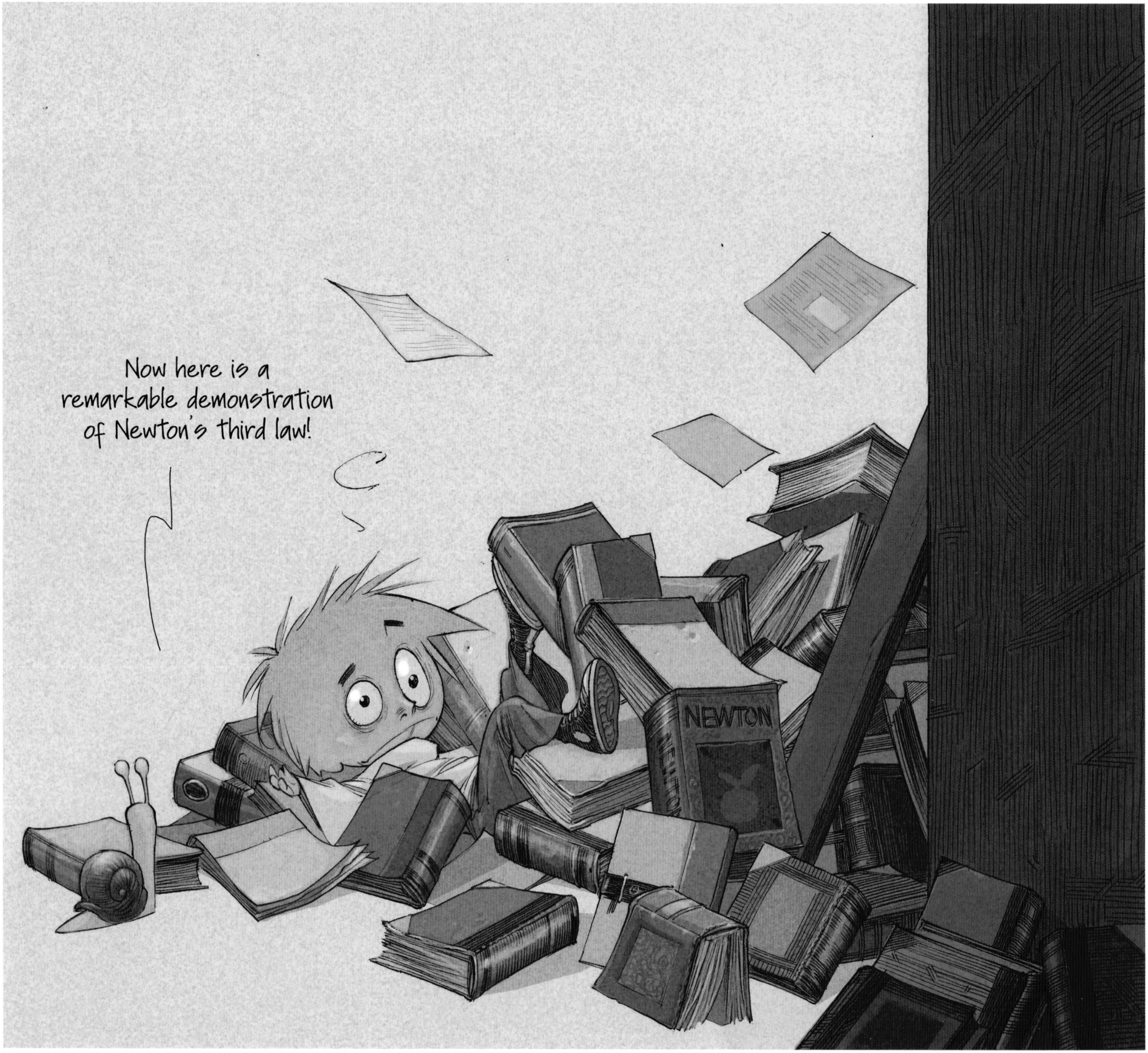
Now here is a remarkable demonstration of Newton's third law!
NEWTON

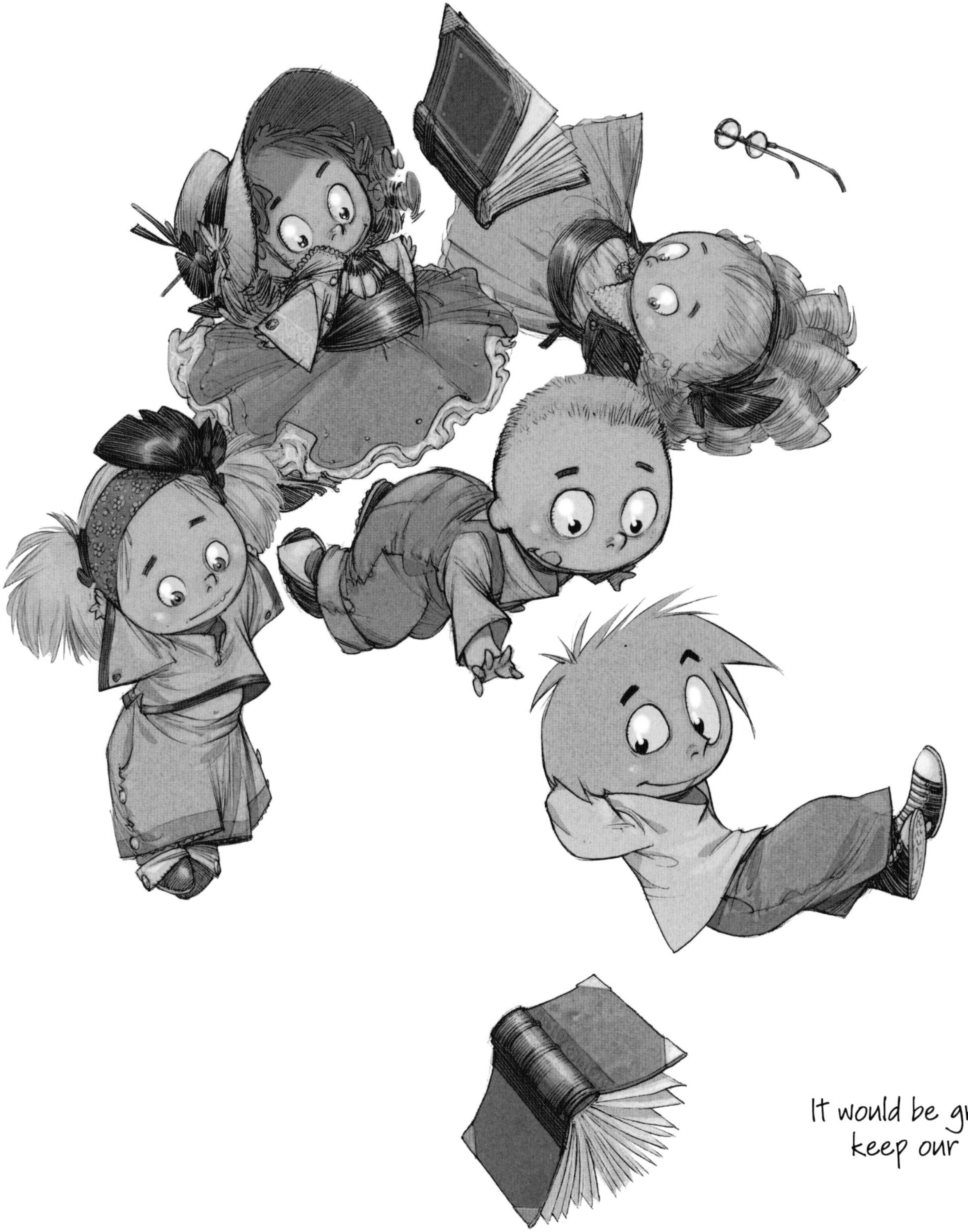

It would be great if we didn't have to keep our feet on the ground...

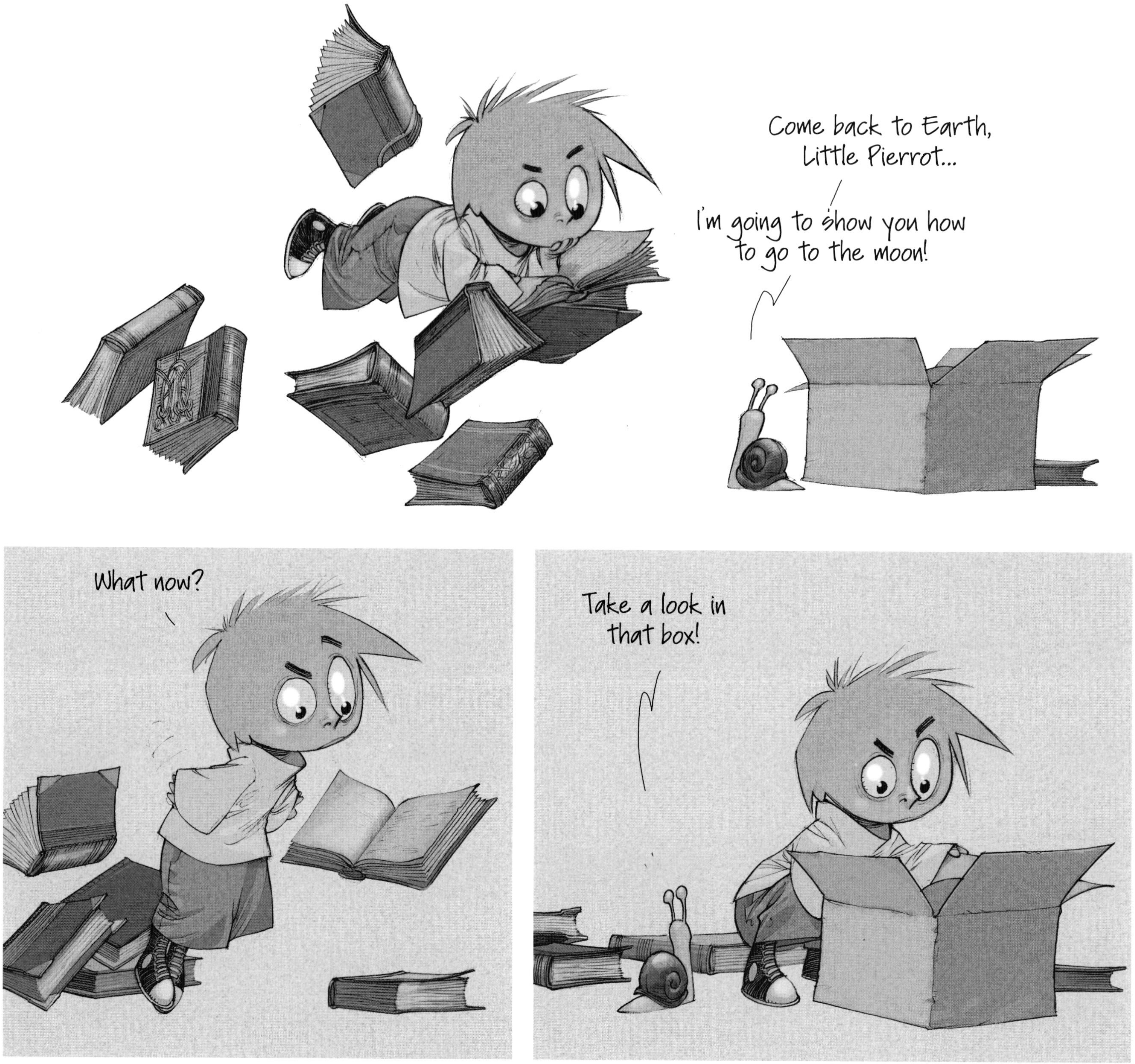
Come back to Earth, Little Pierrot...
I'm going to show you how to go to the moon!
What now?
Take a look in that box!

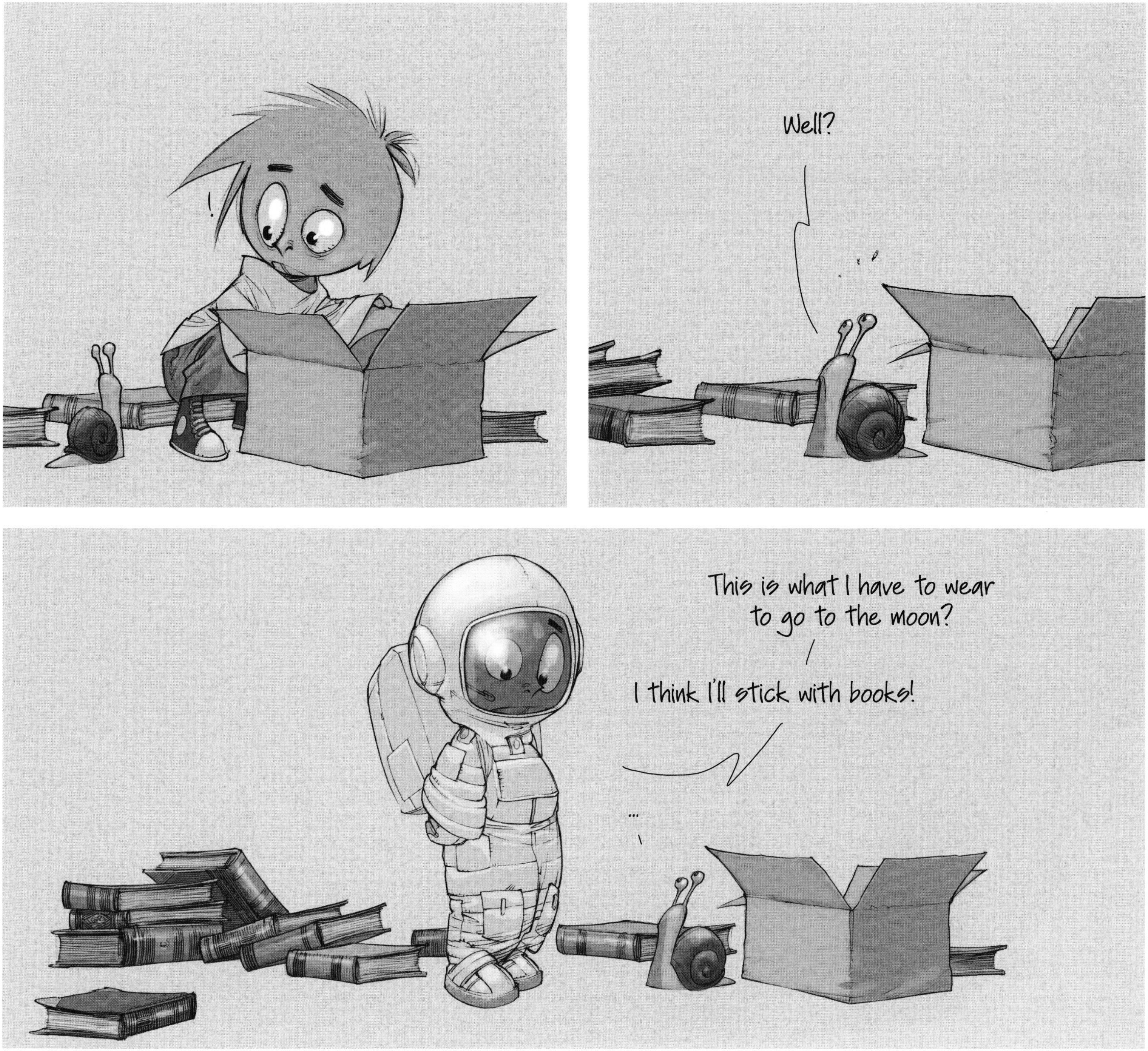
!
Well?
This is what I have to wear to go to the moon?
I think I'll stick with books!
...

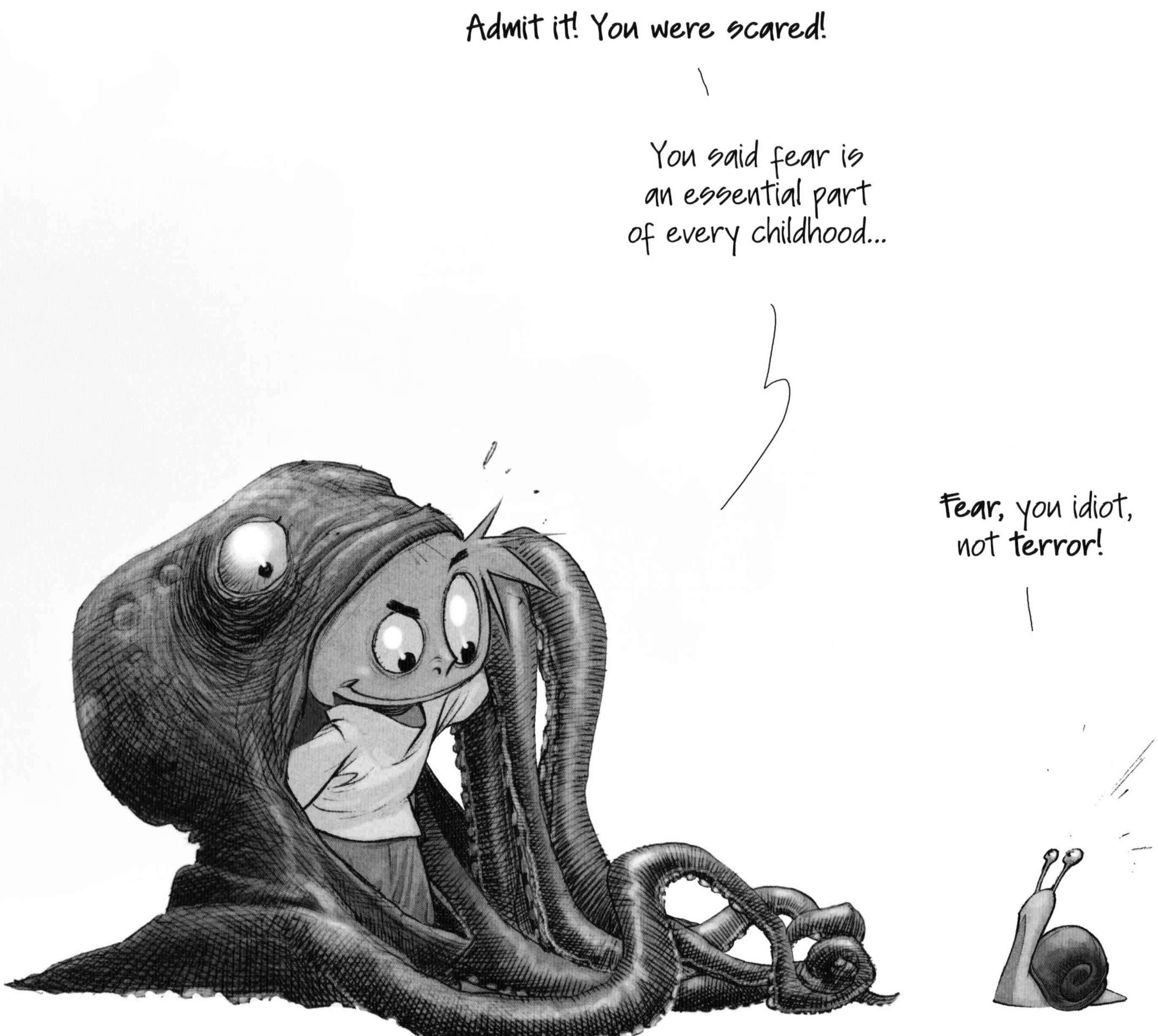
Admit it! You were scared!
You said fear is an essential part of every childhood...
Fear, you idiot, not terror!

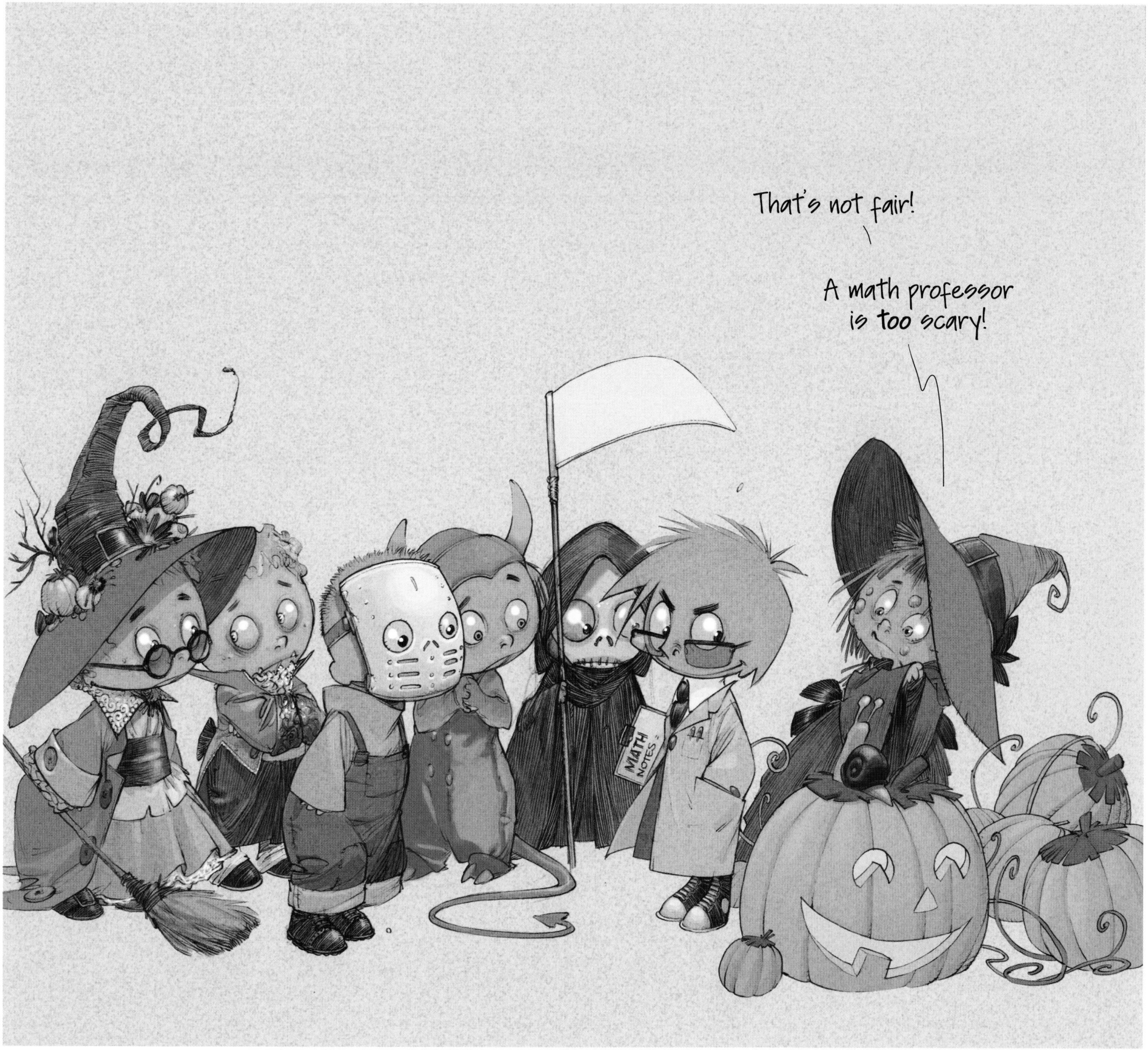
That's not fair!
A math professor
is too scary!

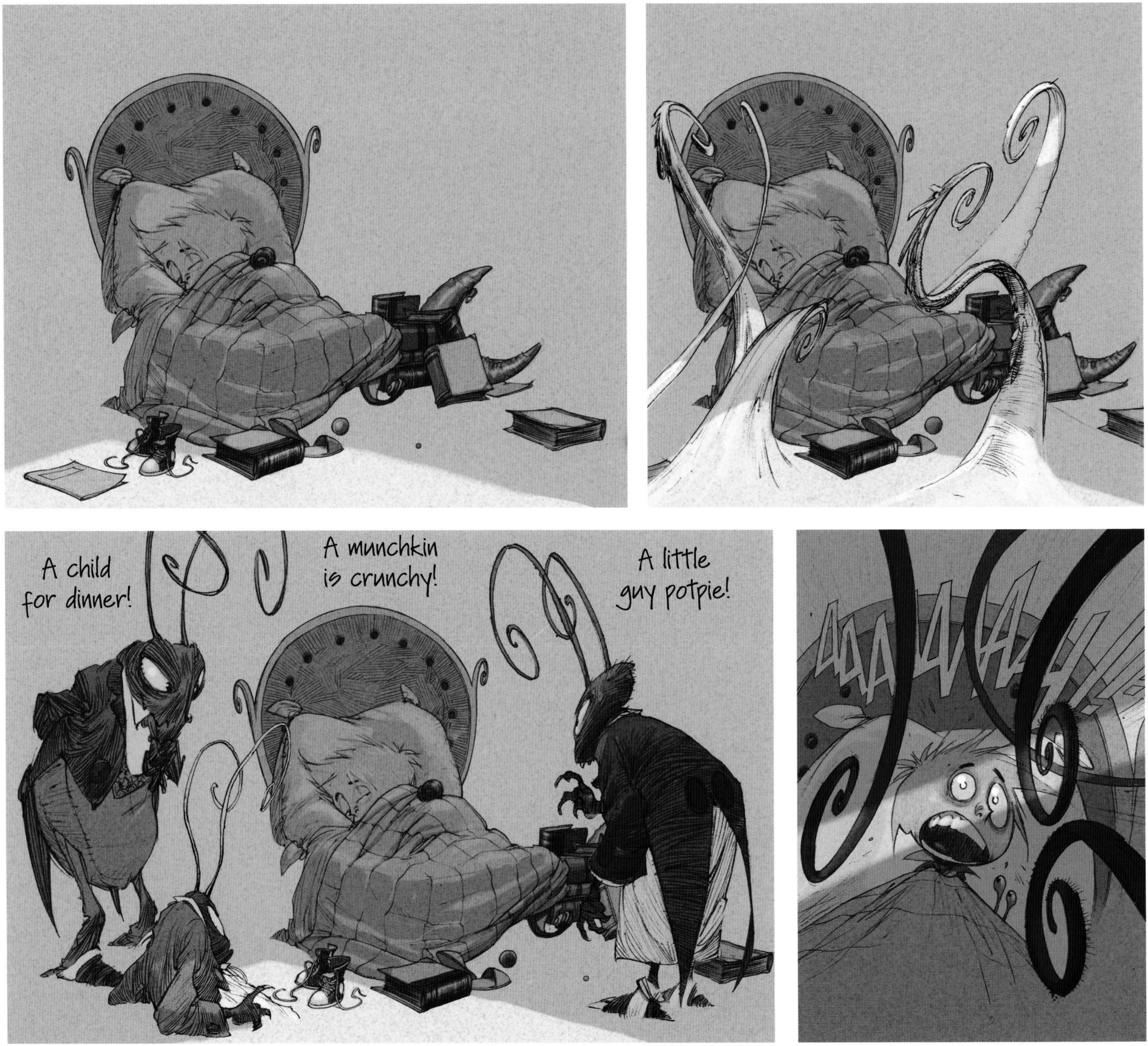
A child for dinner!
A munchkin is crunchy!
A little guy potpie!

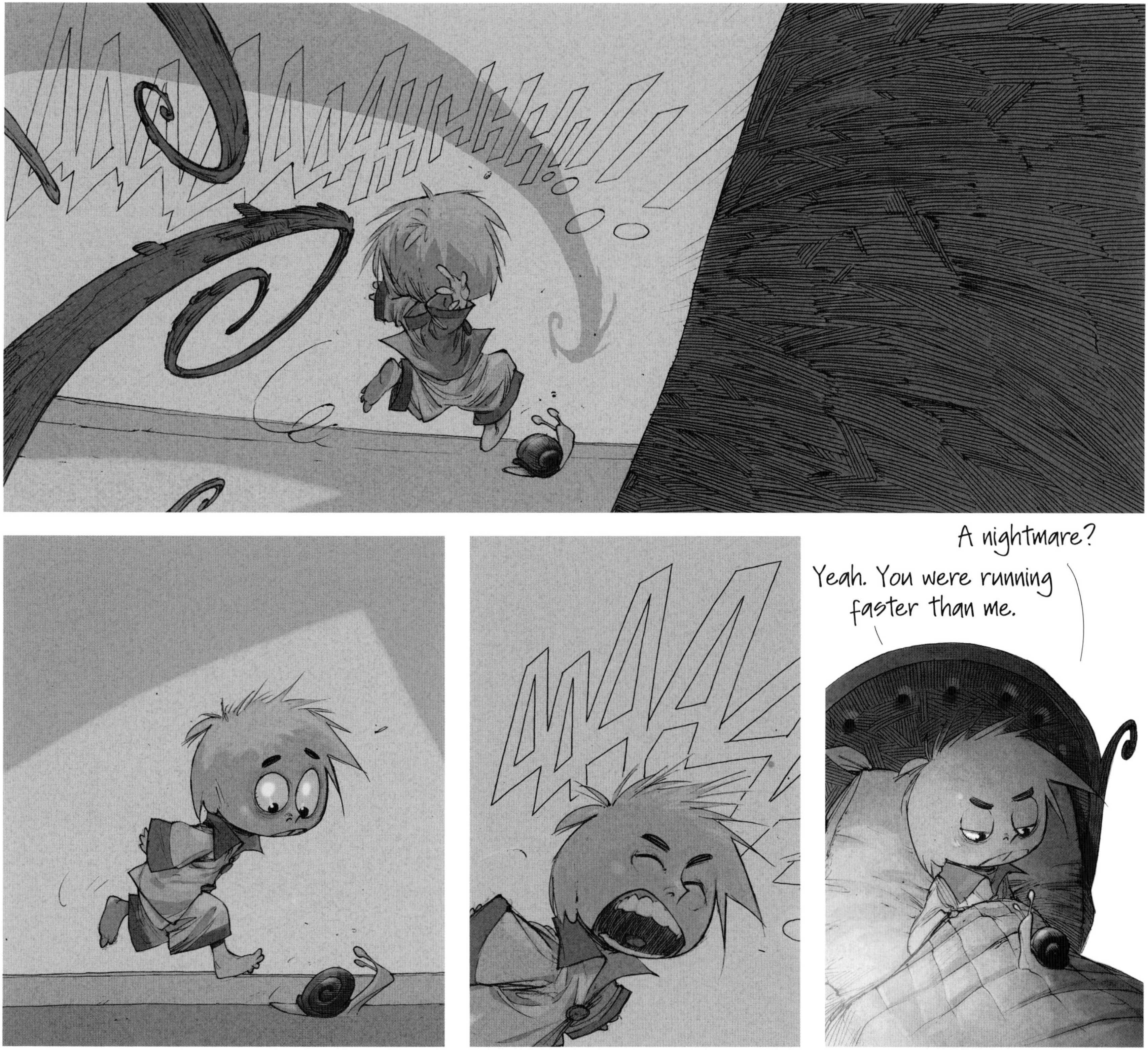
A nightmare?
Yeah. You were running faster than me.

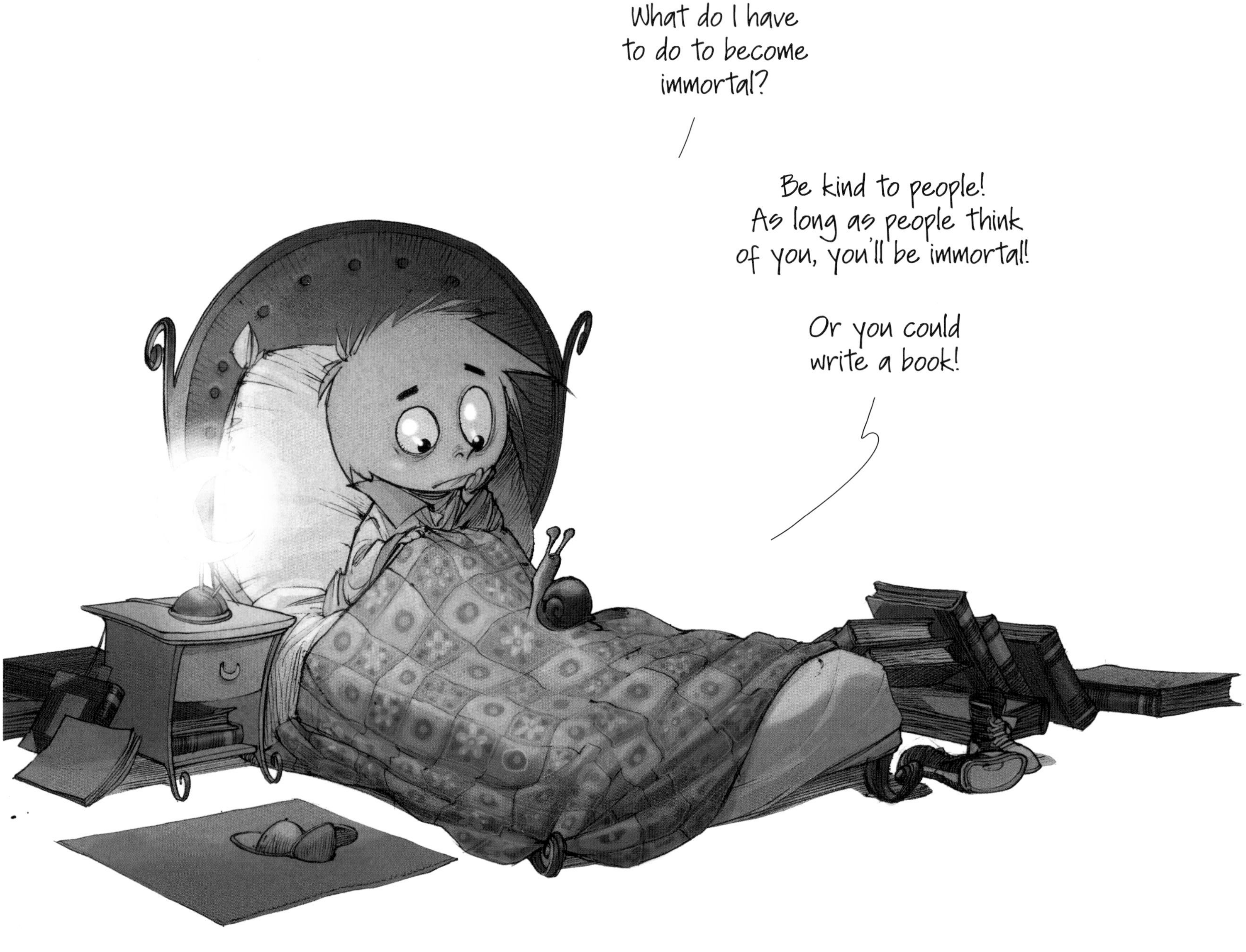
What do I have to do to become immortal?
Be kind to people! As long as people think of you, you'll be immortal!
Or you could write a book!

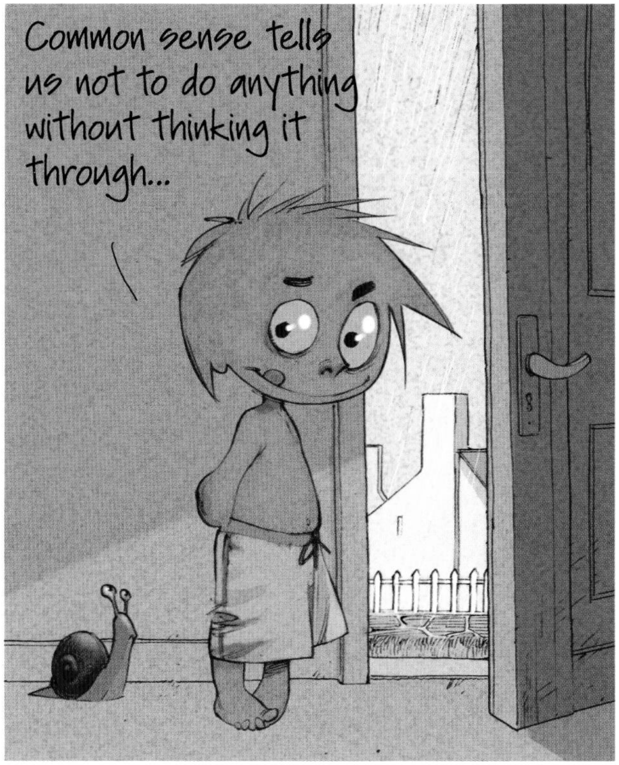
Common sense tells us not to do anything without thinking it through...

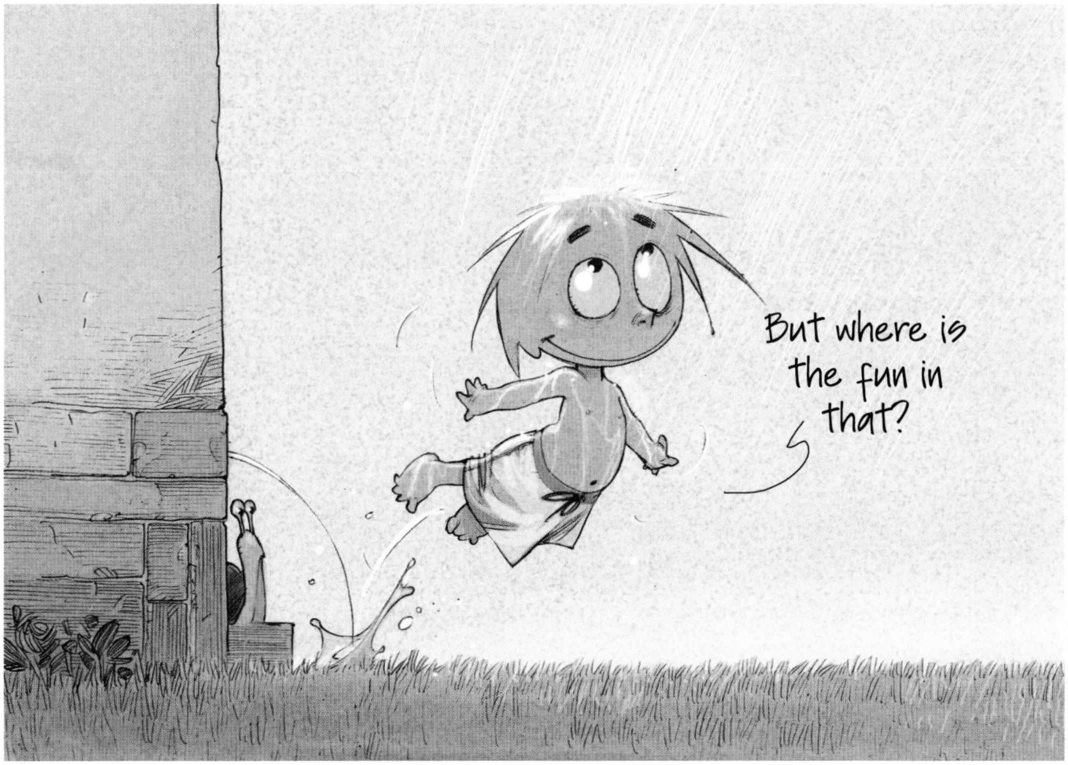
But where is the fun in that?

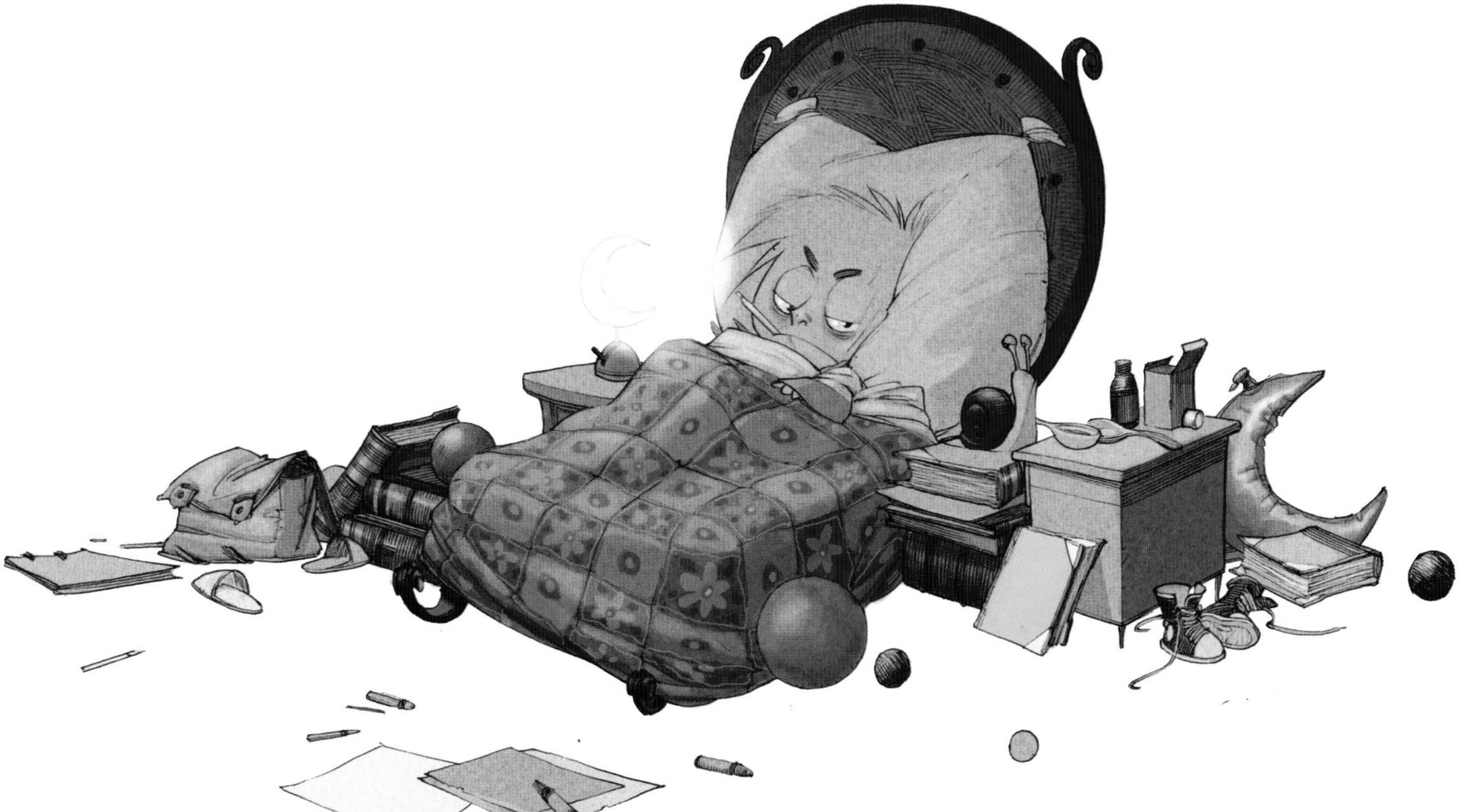

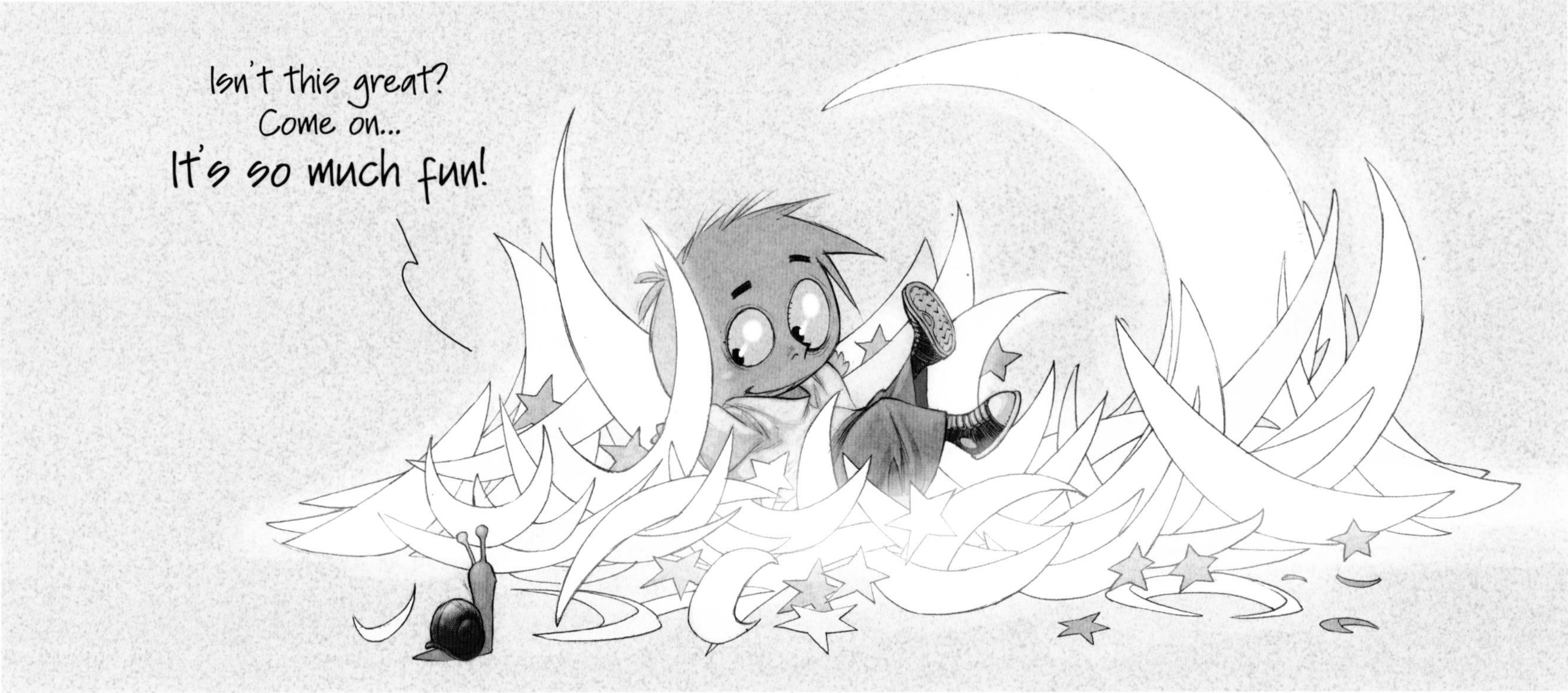
Isn't this great?
Come on...
It's so much fun!

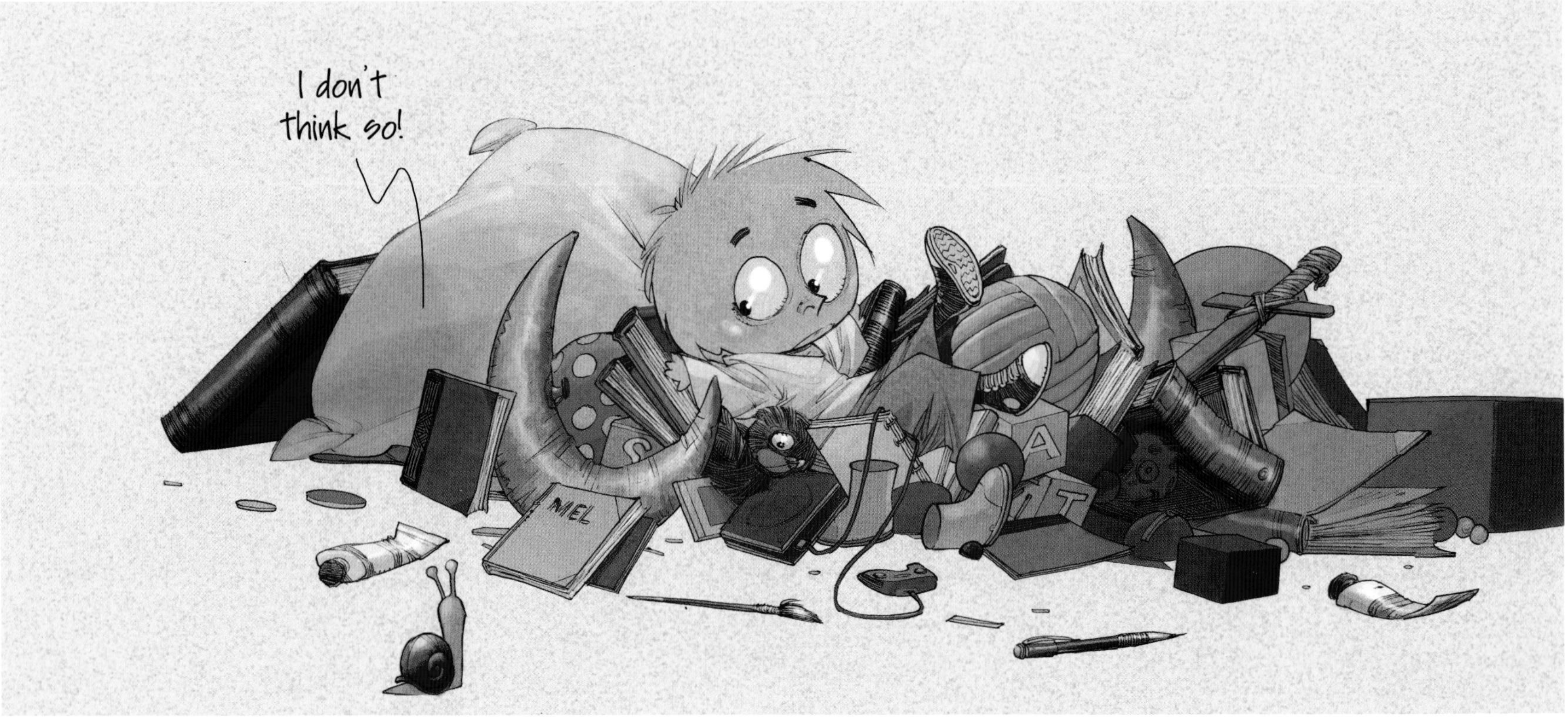
I don't
think so!
MEL

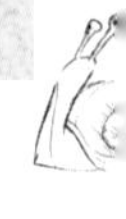

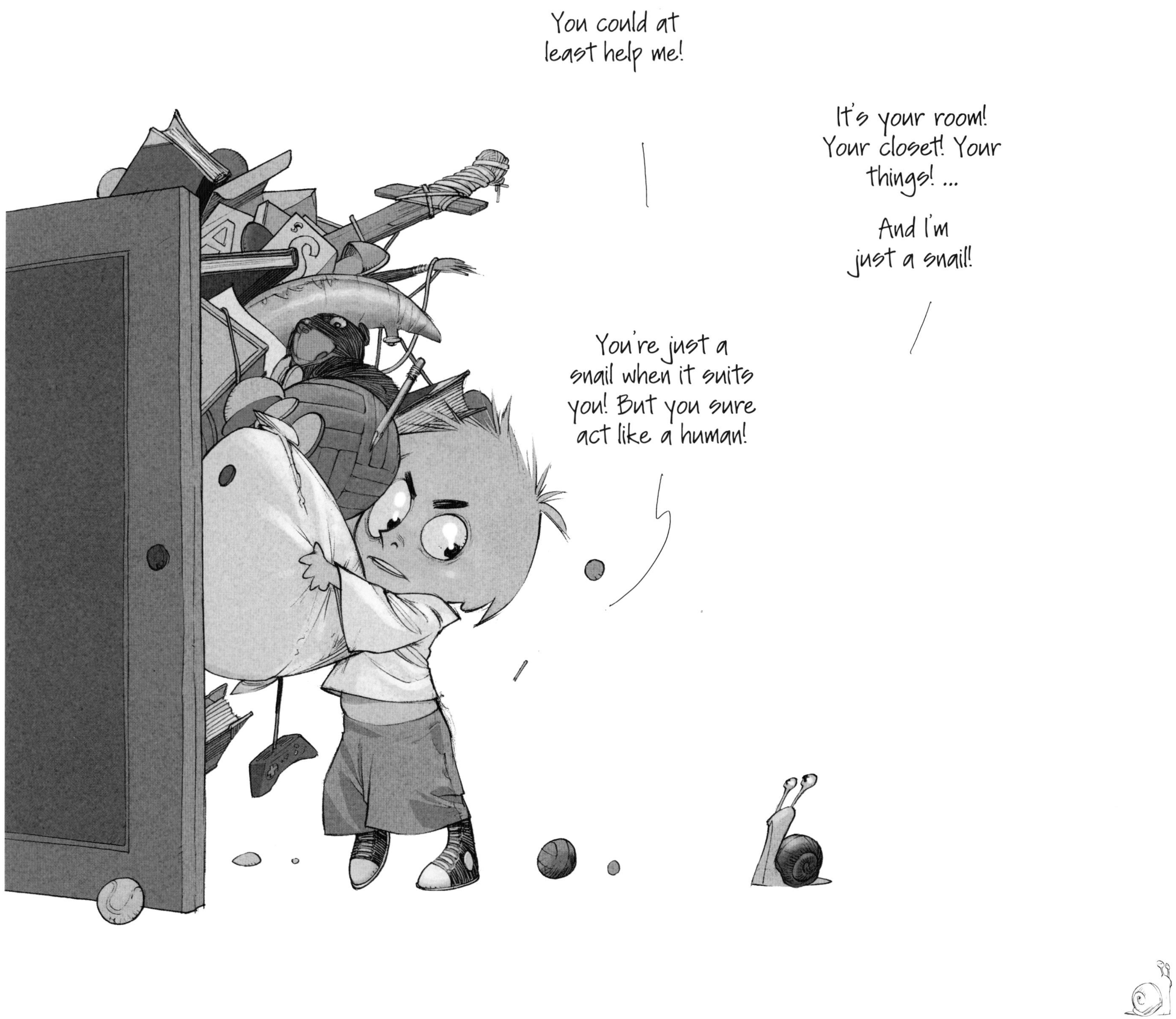
You could at least help me!
It's your room! Your closet! Your things! ...
And I'm just a snail!
You're just a snail when it suits you! But you sure act like a human!

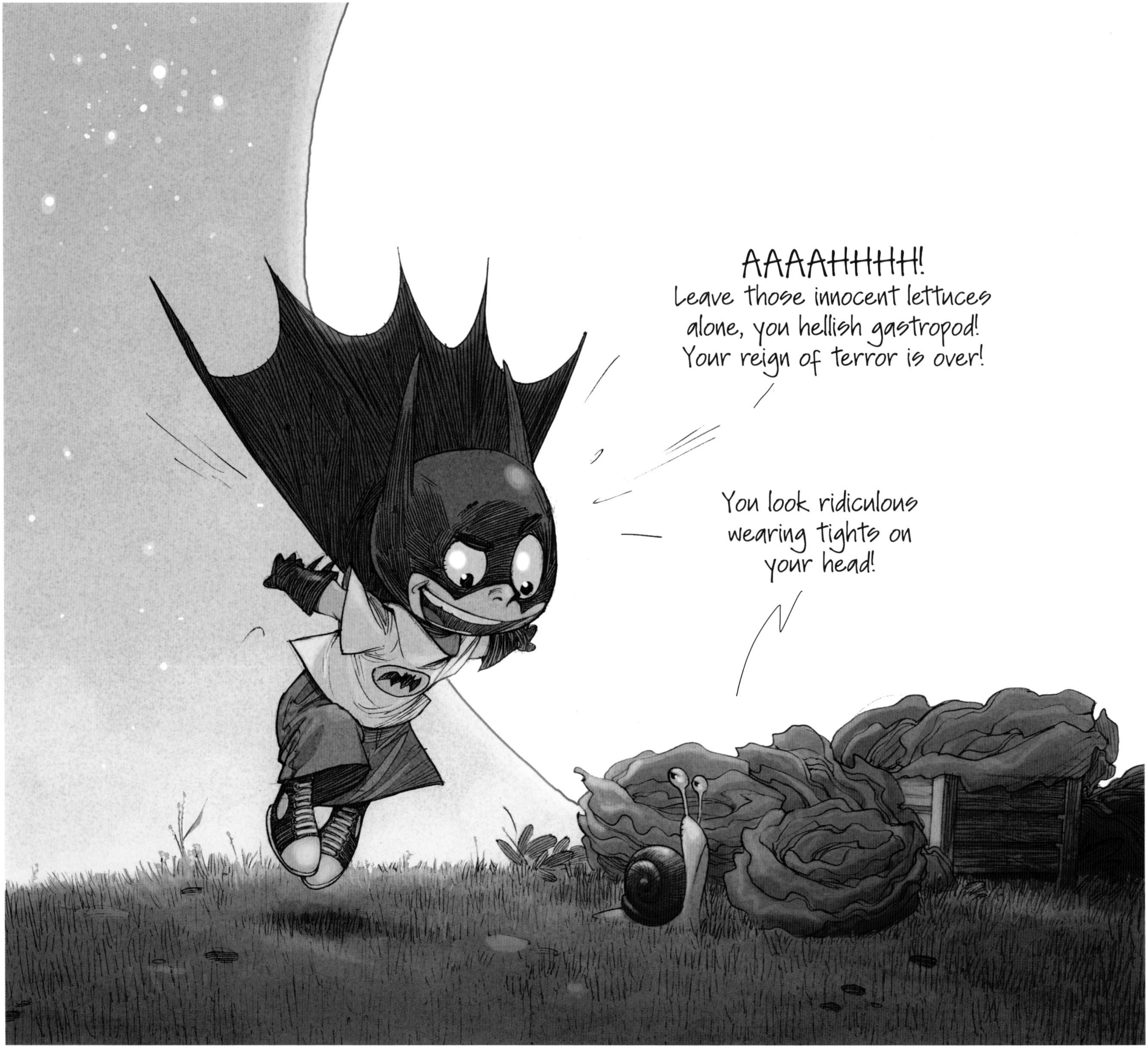
AAAAHHHH!
Leave those innocent lettuces alone, you hellish gastropod! Your reign of terror is over!
You look ridiculous wearing tights on your head!

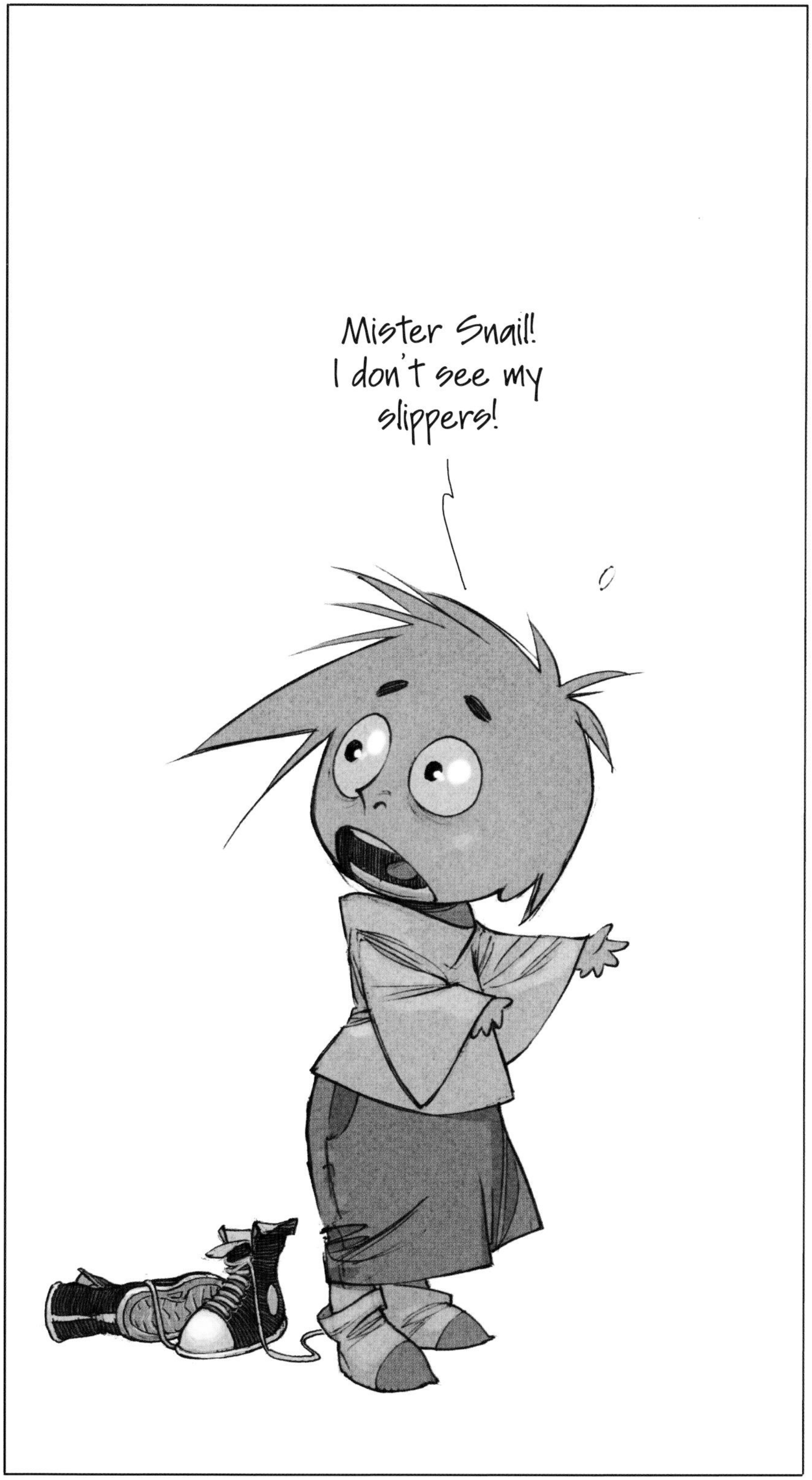
Mister Snail!
I don't see my slippers!

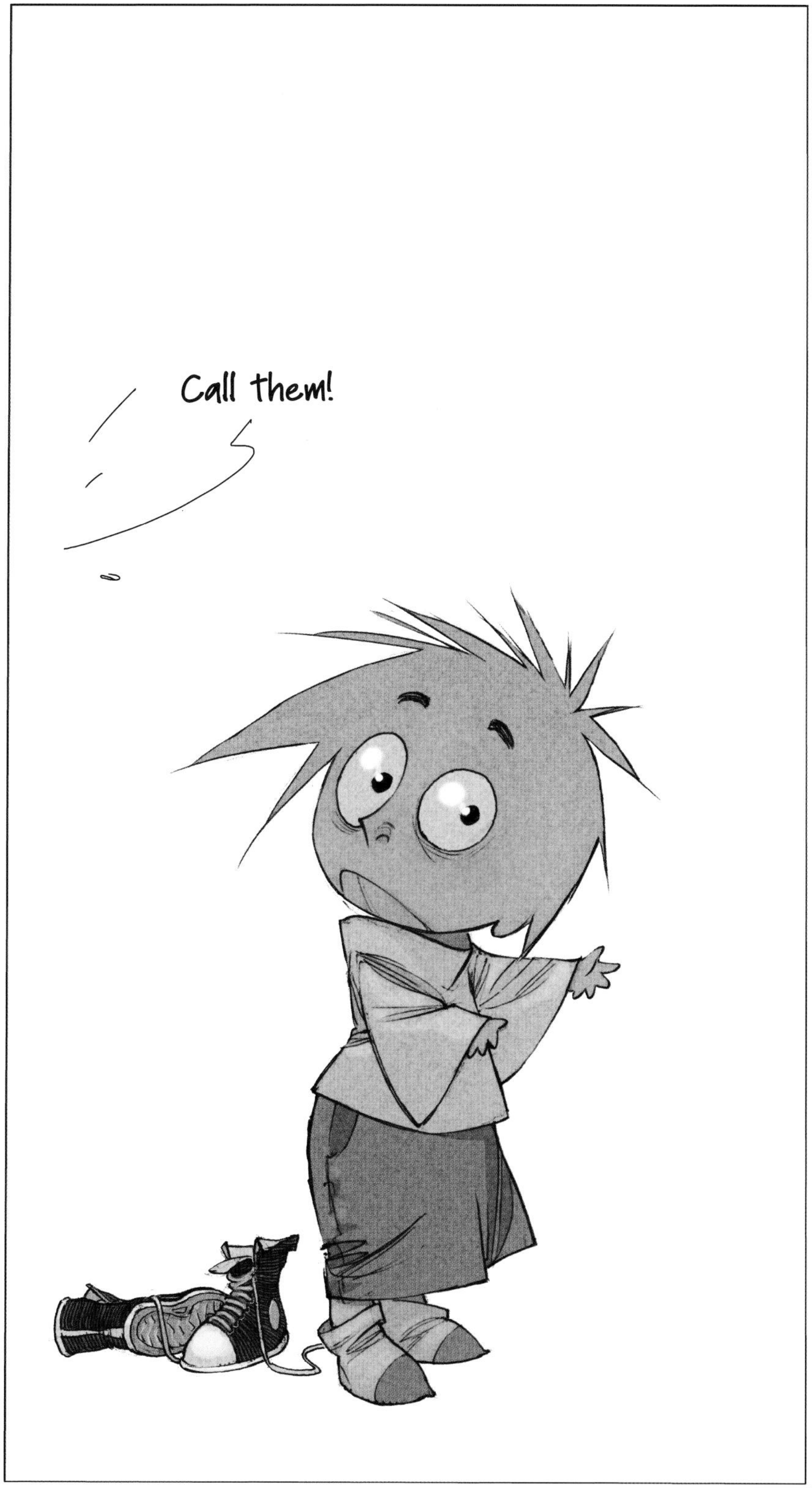
Call them!

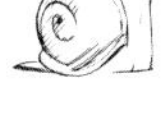

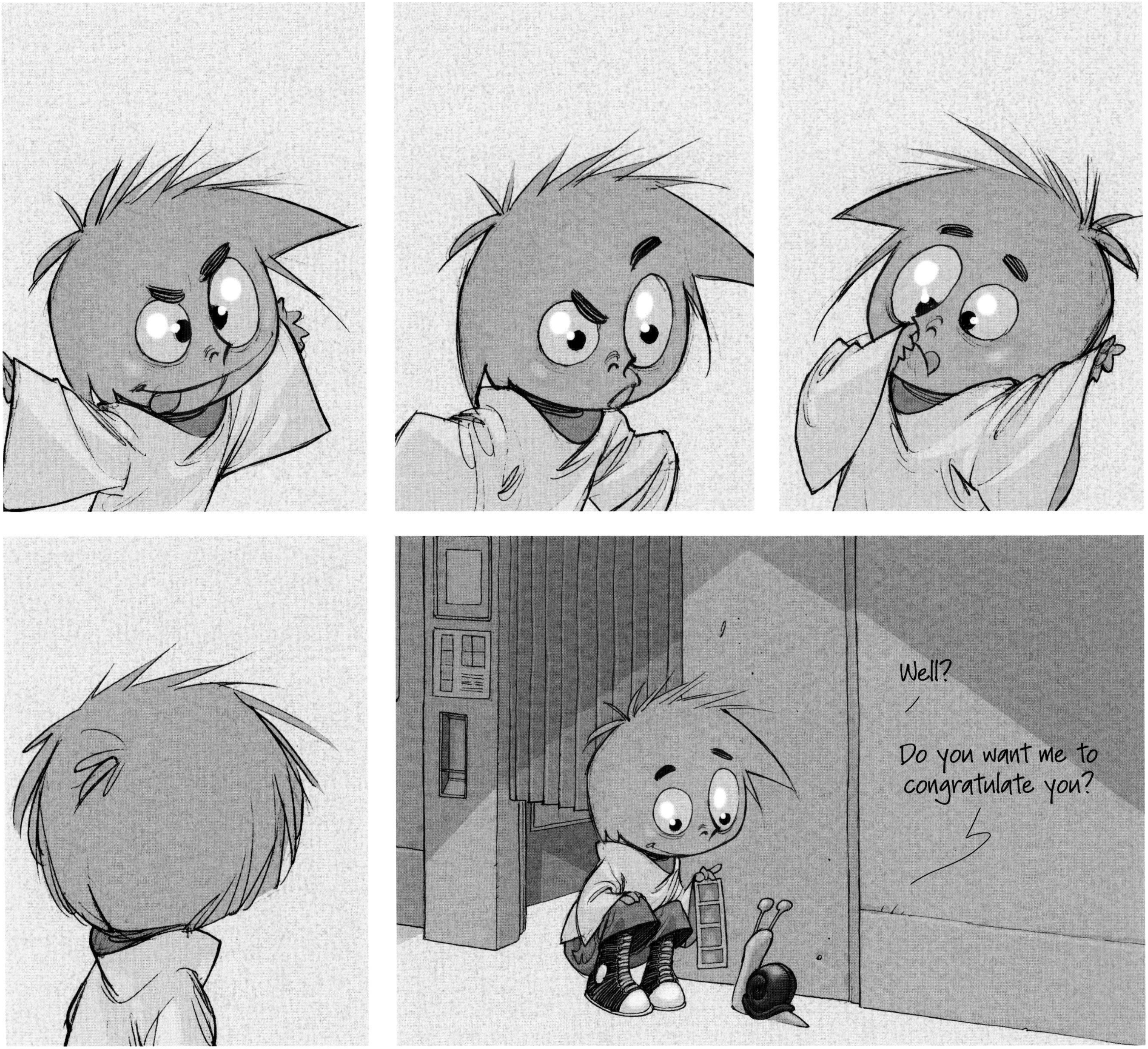
Well?
Do you want me to congratulate you?

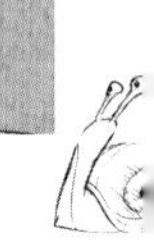

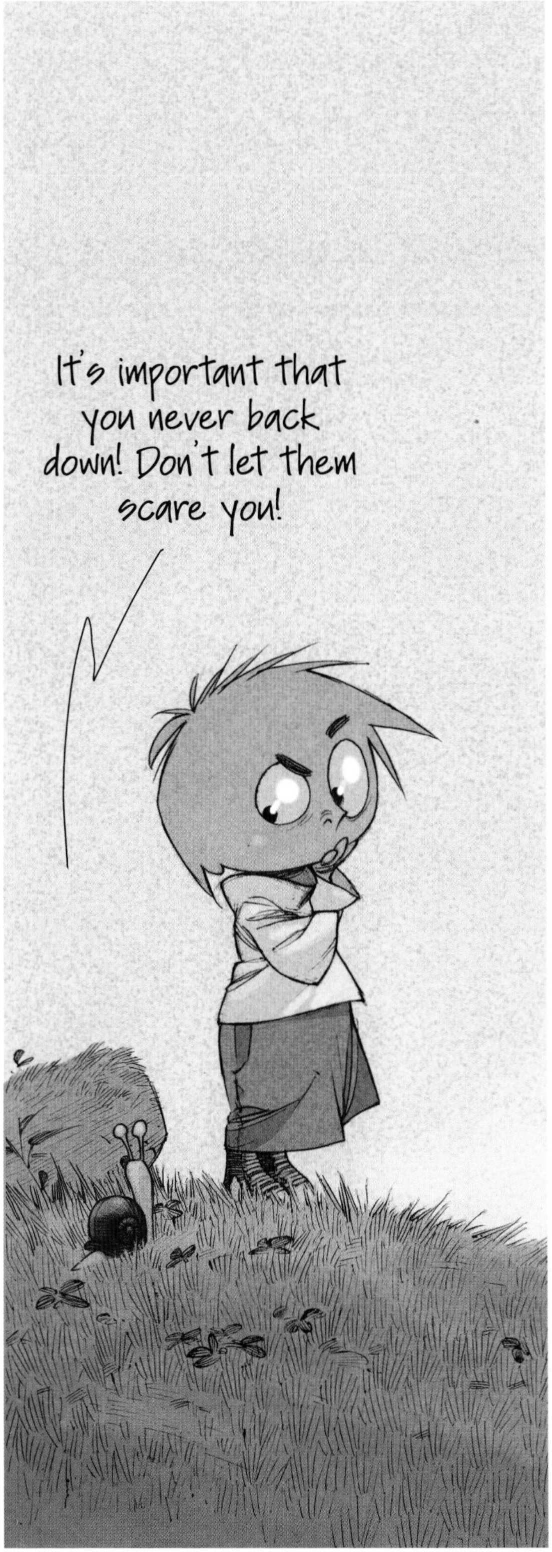
It's important that you never back down! Don't let them scare you!

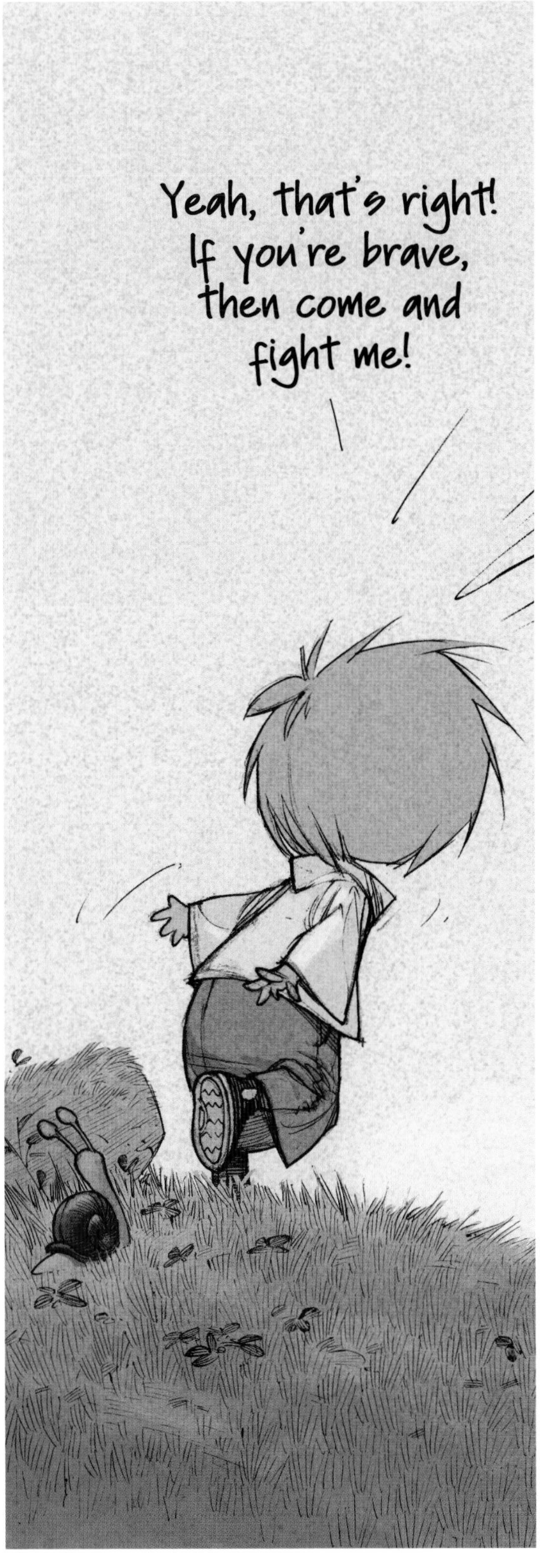
Yeah, that's right! If you're brave, then come and fight me!

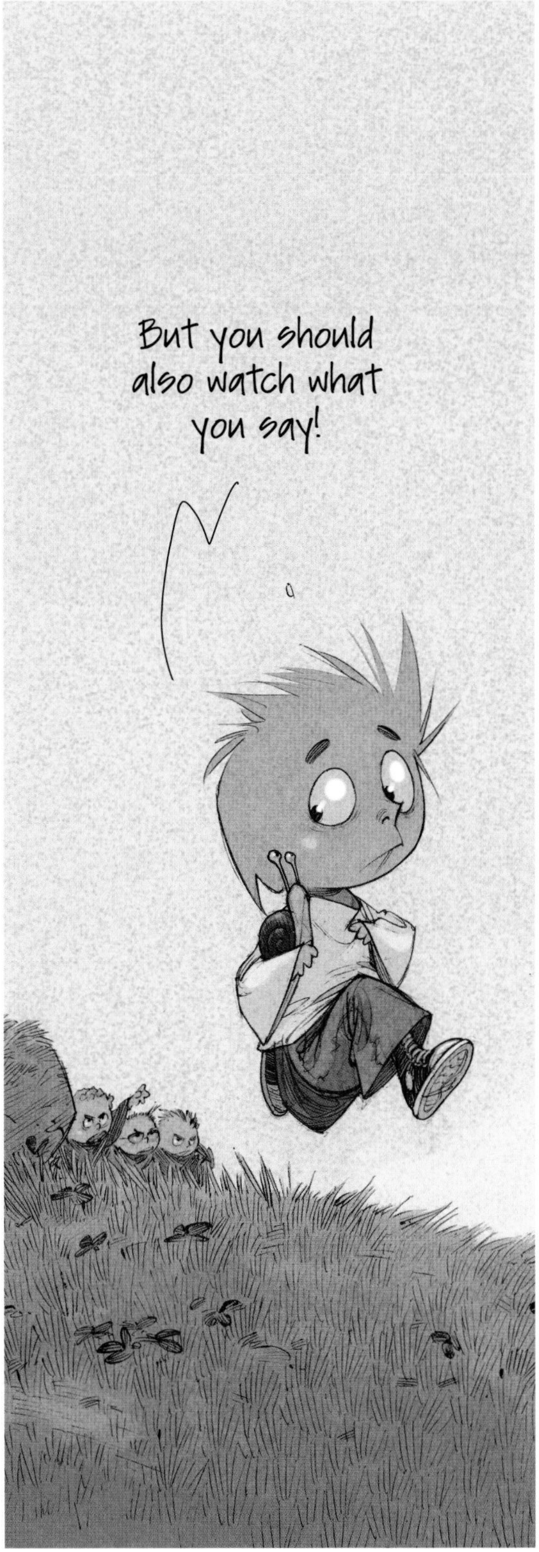
But you should also watch what you say!

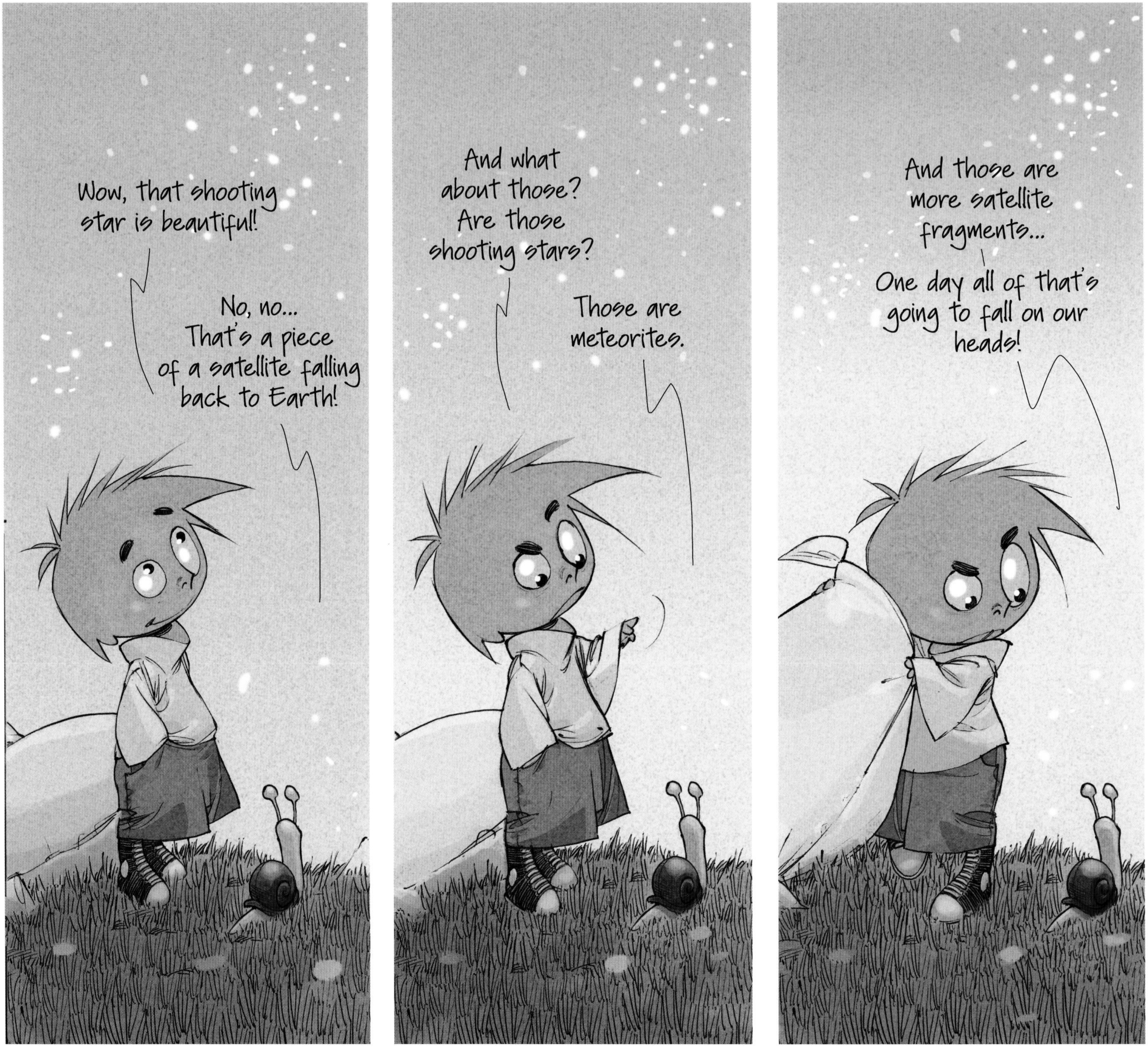
Wow, that shooting star is beautiful!
No, no... That's a piece of a satellite falling back to Earth!
And what about those? Are those shooting stars?
Those are meteorites.
And those are more satellite fragments...
One day all of that's going to fall on our heads!

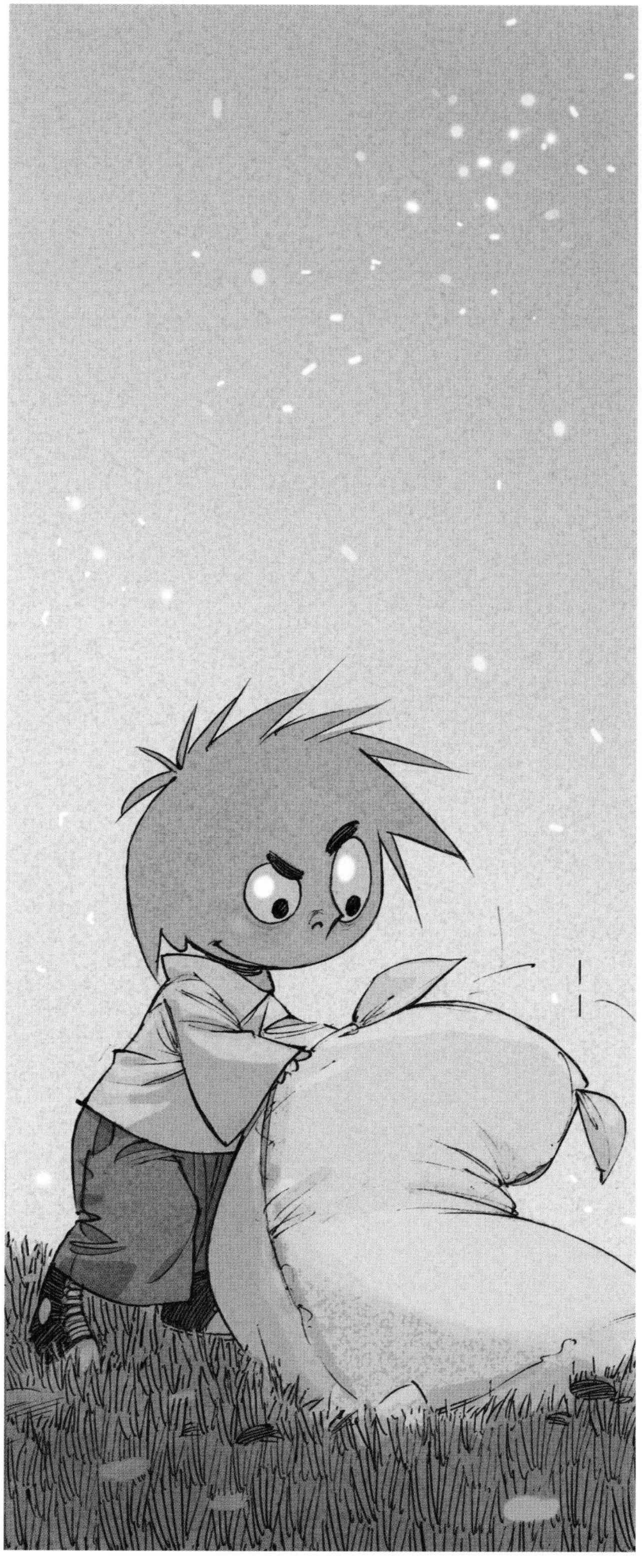

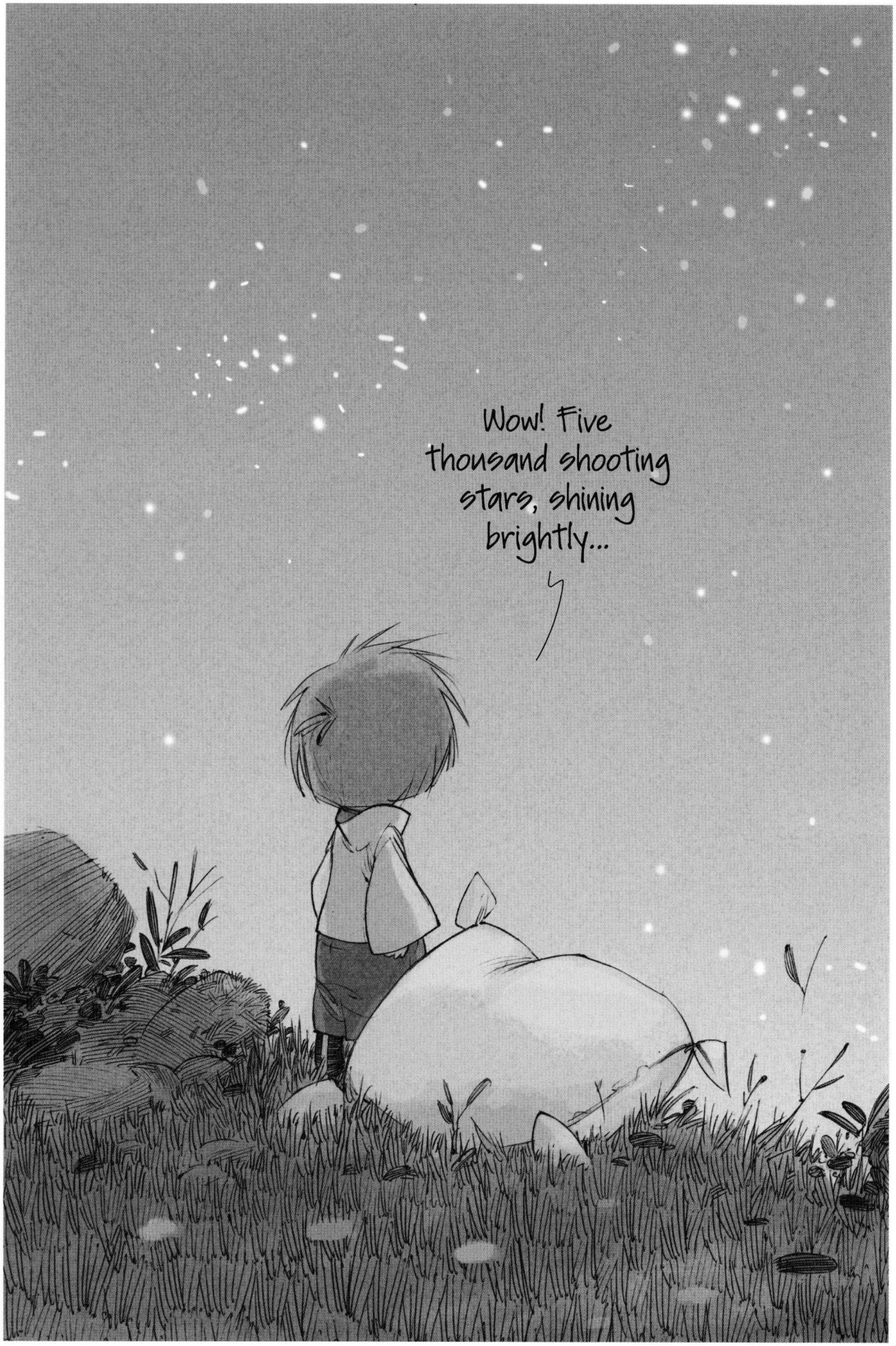
Wow! Five thousand shooting stars, shining brightly...

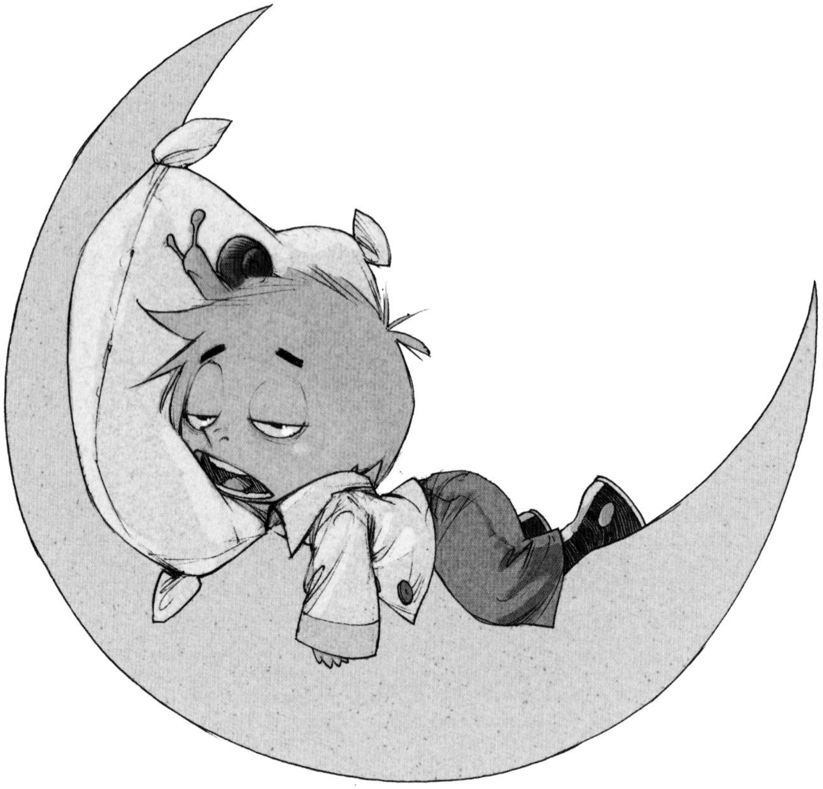

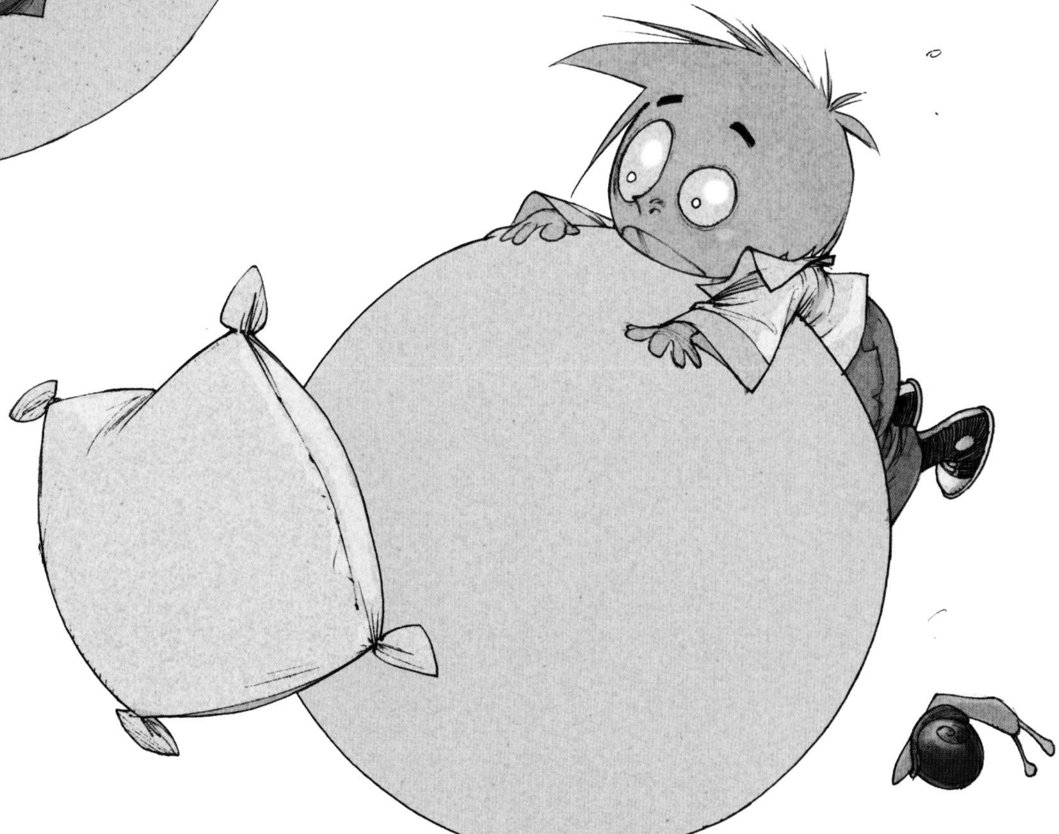

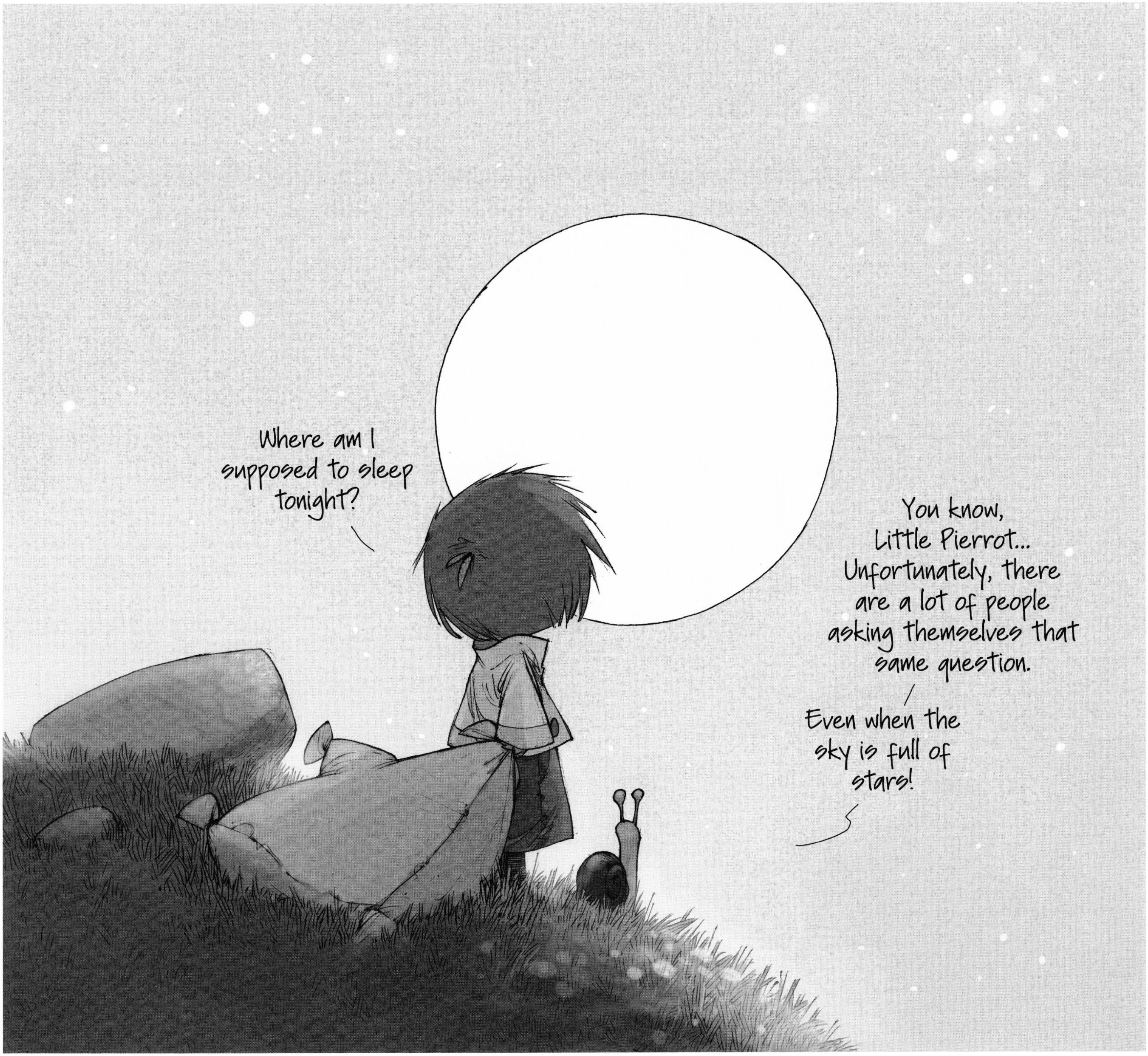
Where am I supposed to sleep tonight?
You know, Little Pierrot... Unfortunately, there are a lot of people asking themselves that same question.
Even when the sky is full of stars!

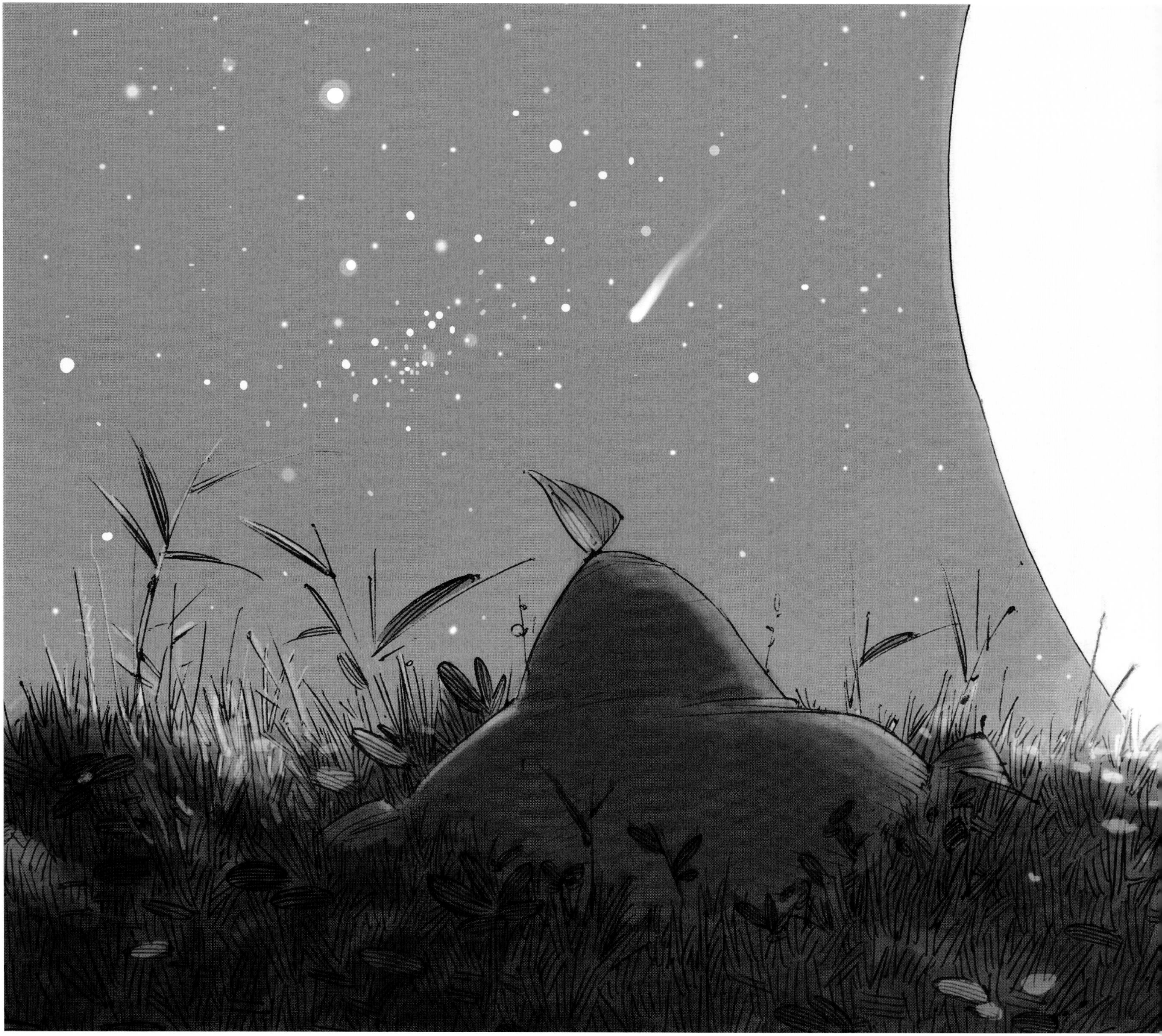

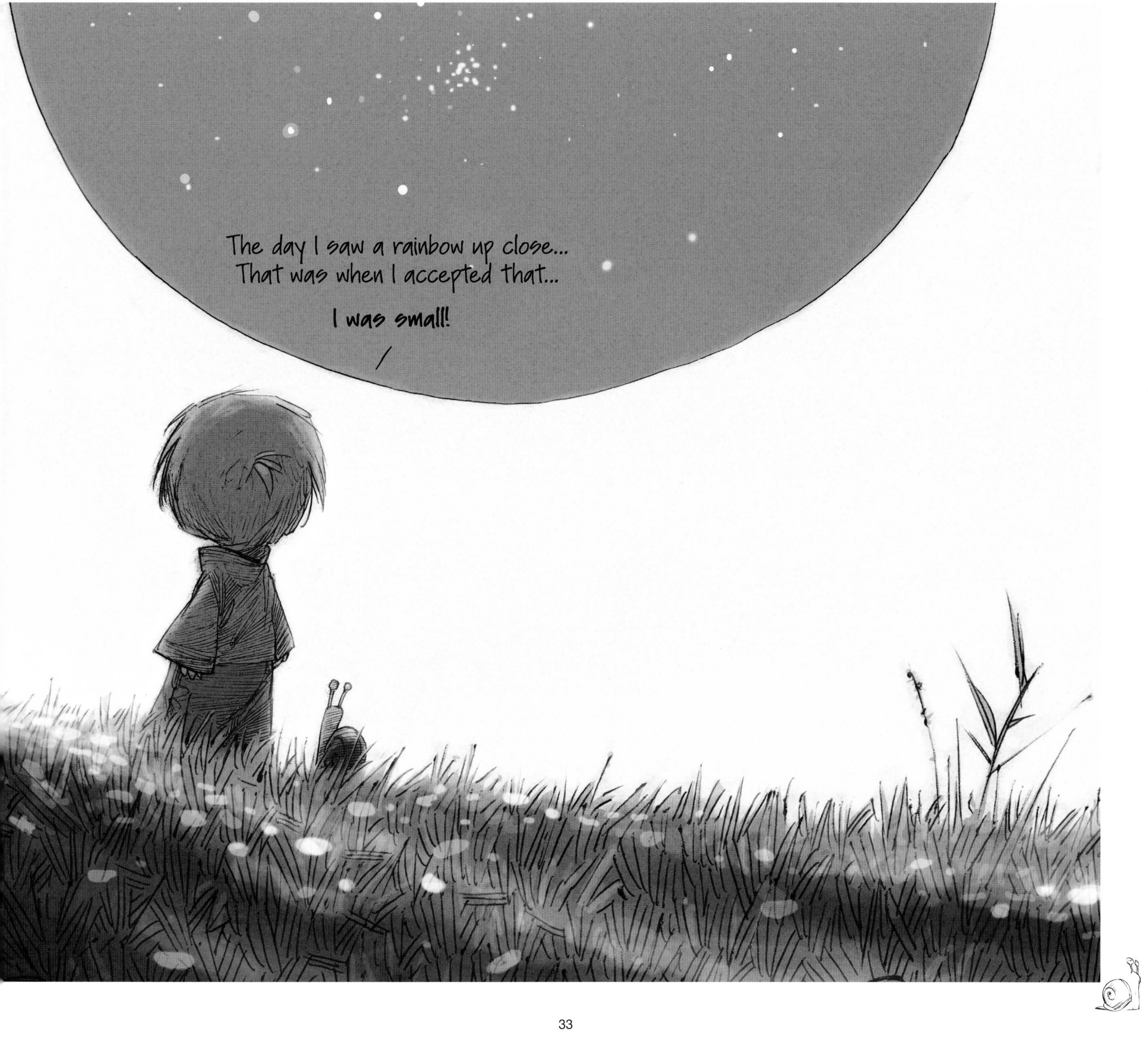
The day I saw a rainbow up close...
That was when I accepted that...
I was small!

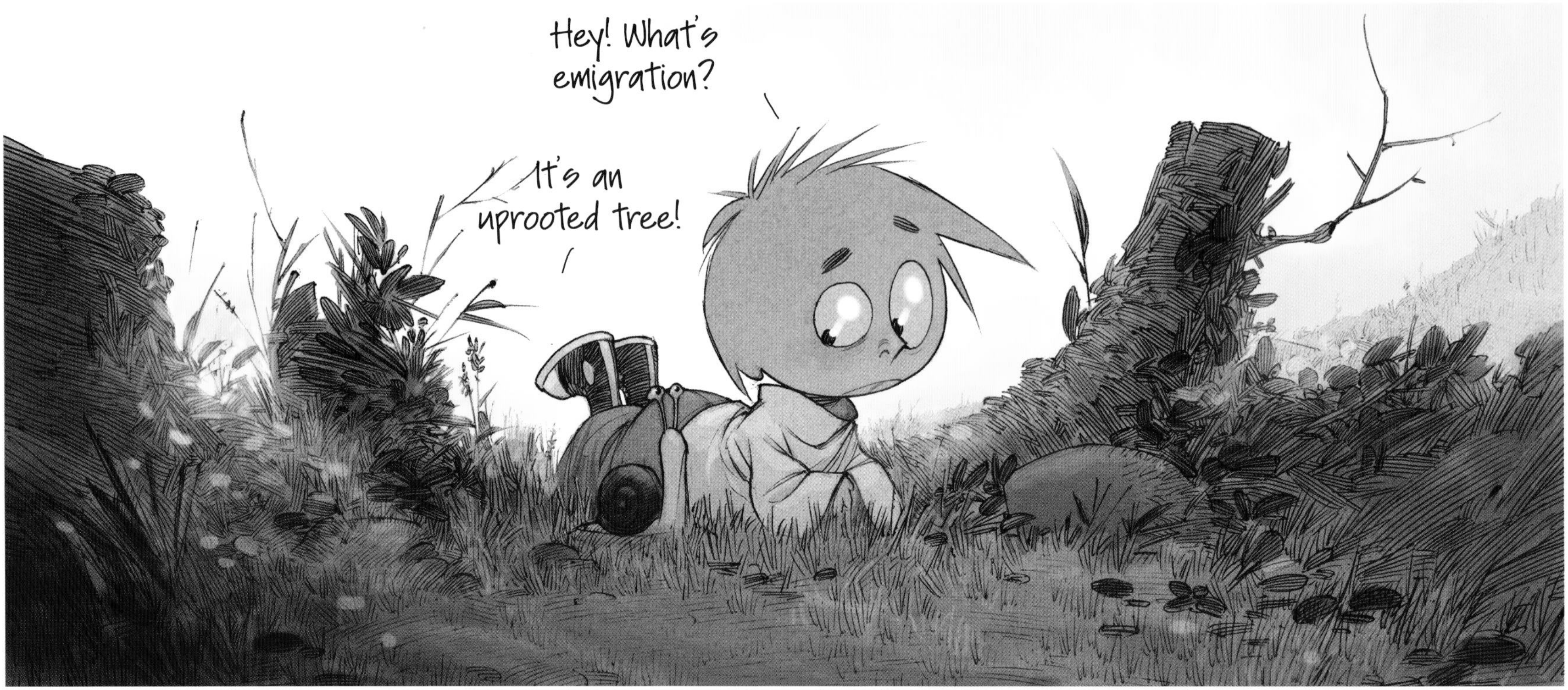
Hey! What's emigration?
It's an uprooted tree!

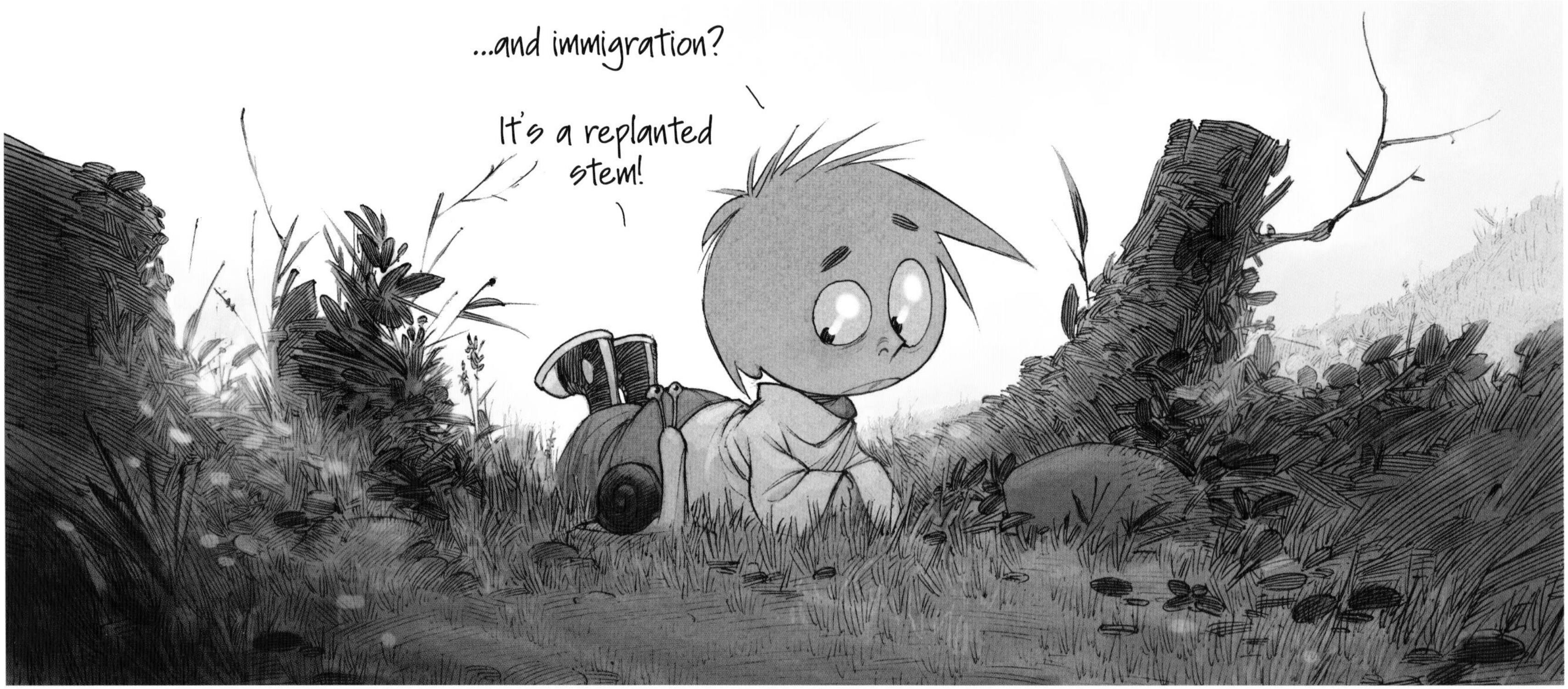
...and immigration?
It's a replanted stem!

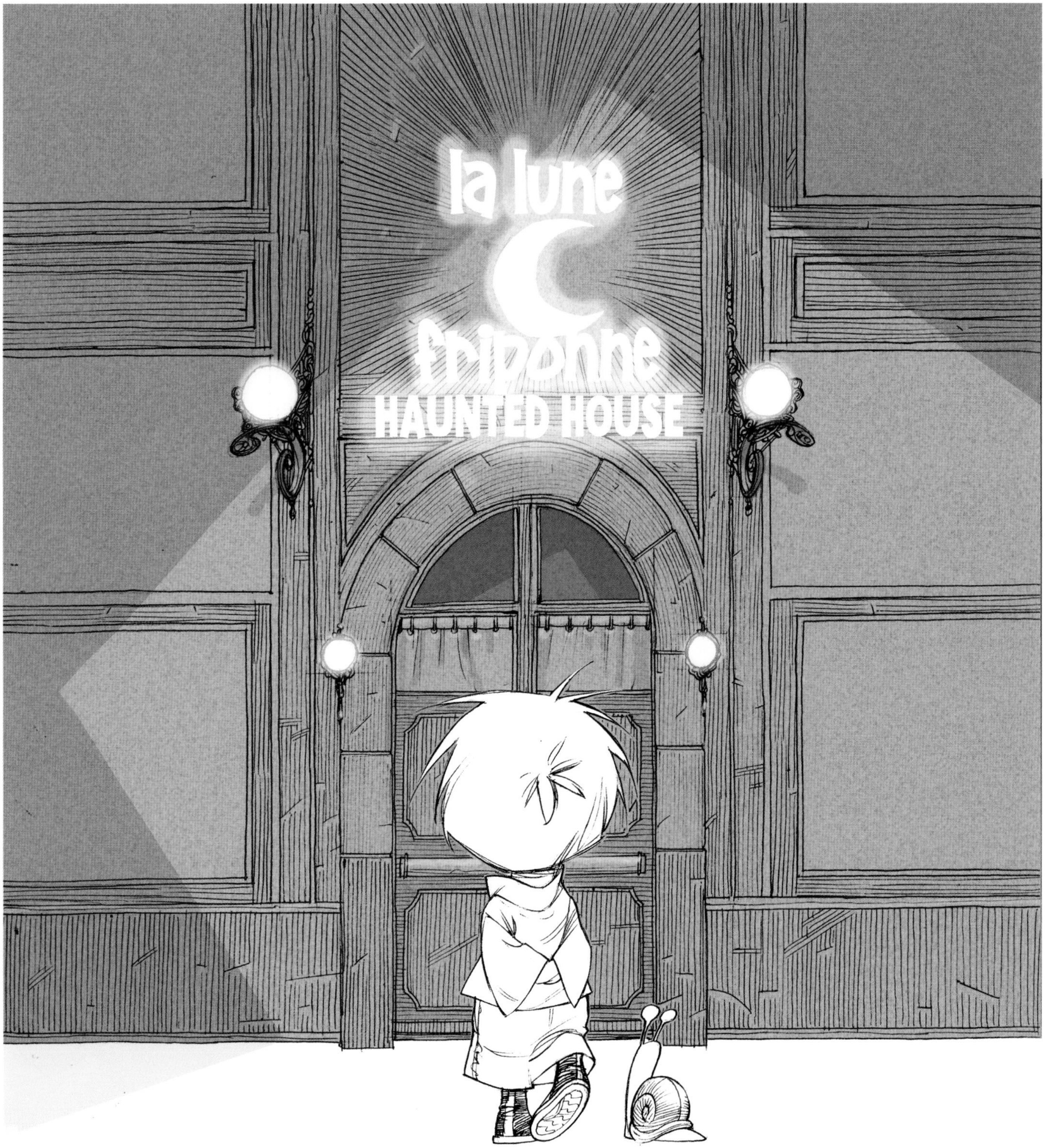
la lune
friponne
HAUNTED HOUSE

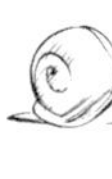

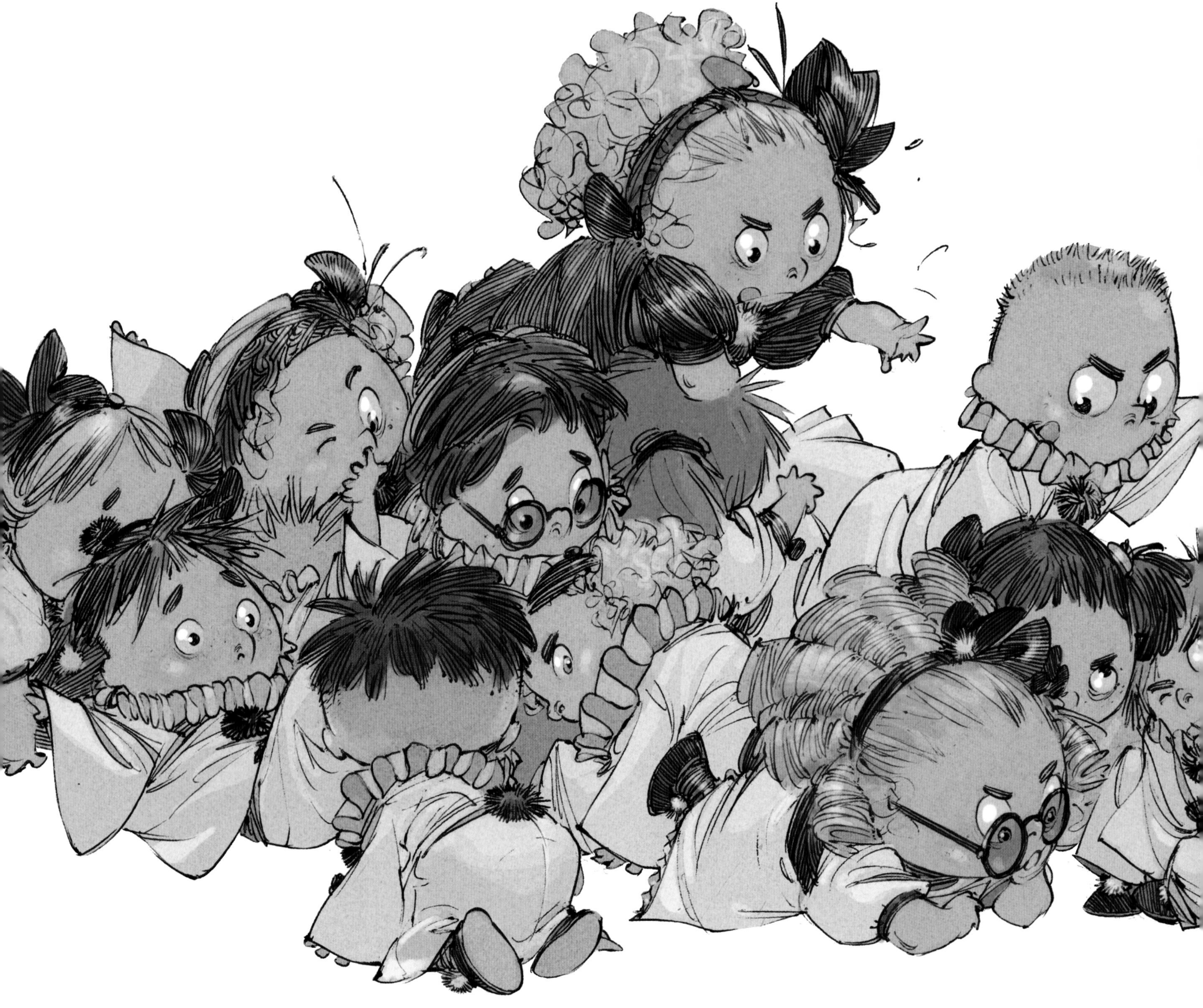

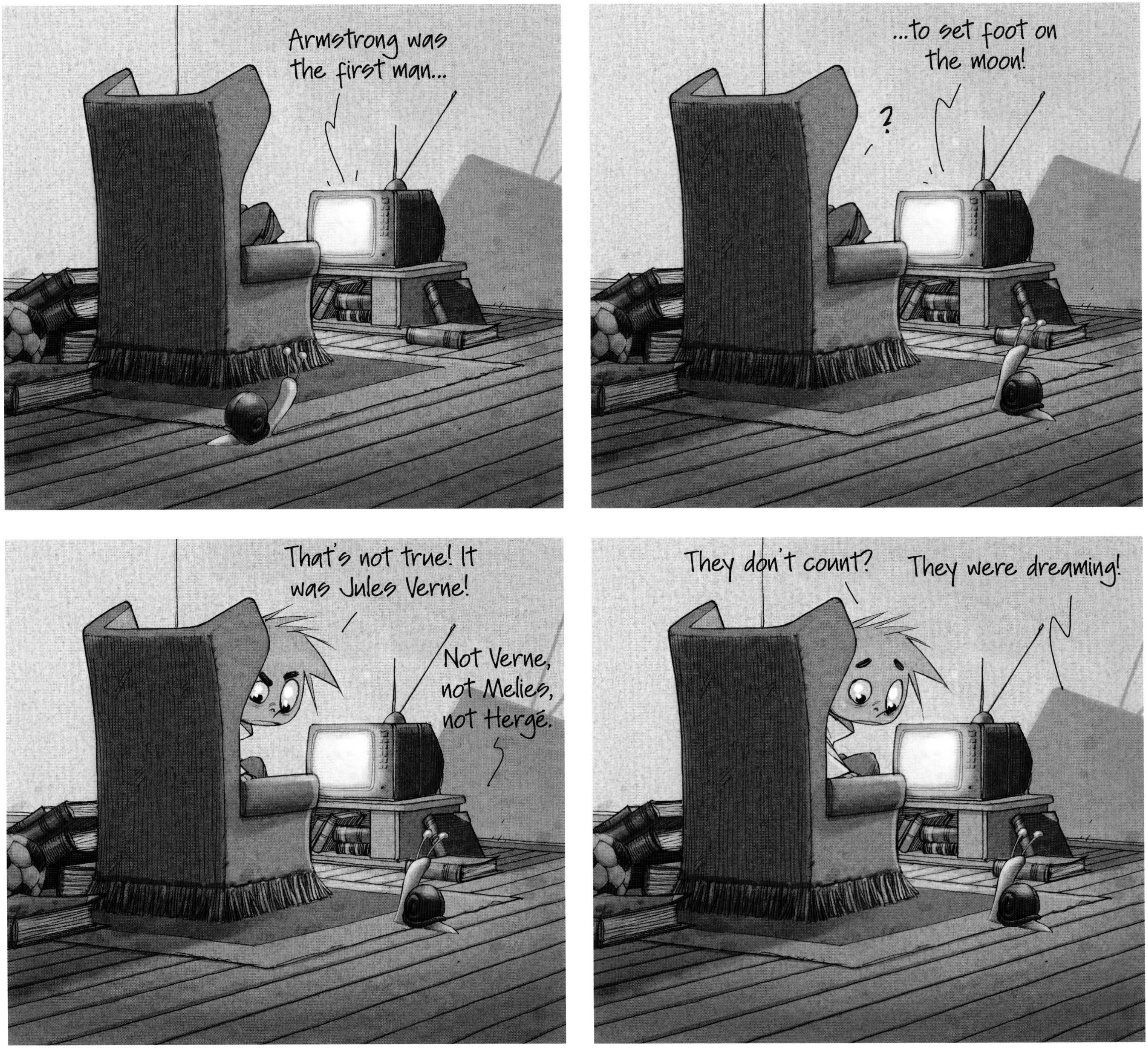
Armstrong was the first man...
...to set foot on the moon!
?
That's not true! It was Jules Verne!
Not Verne, not Melies, not Hergé.
They don't count?
They were dreaming!

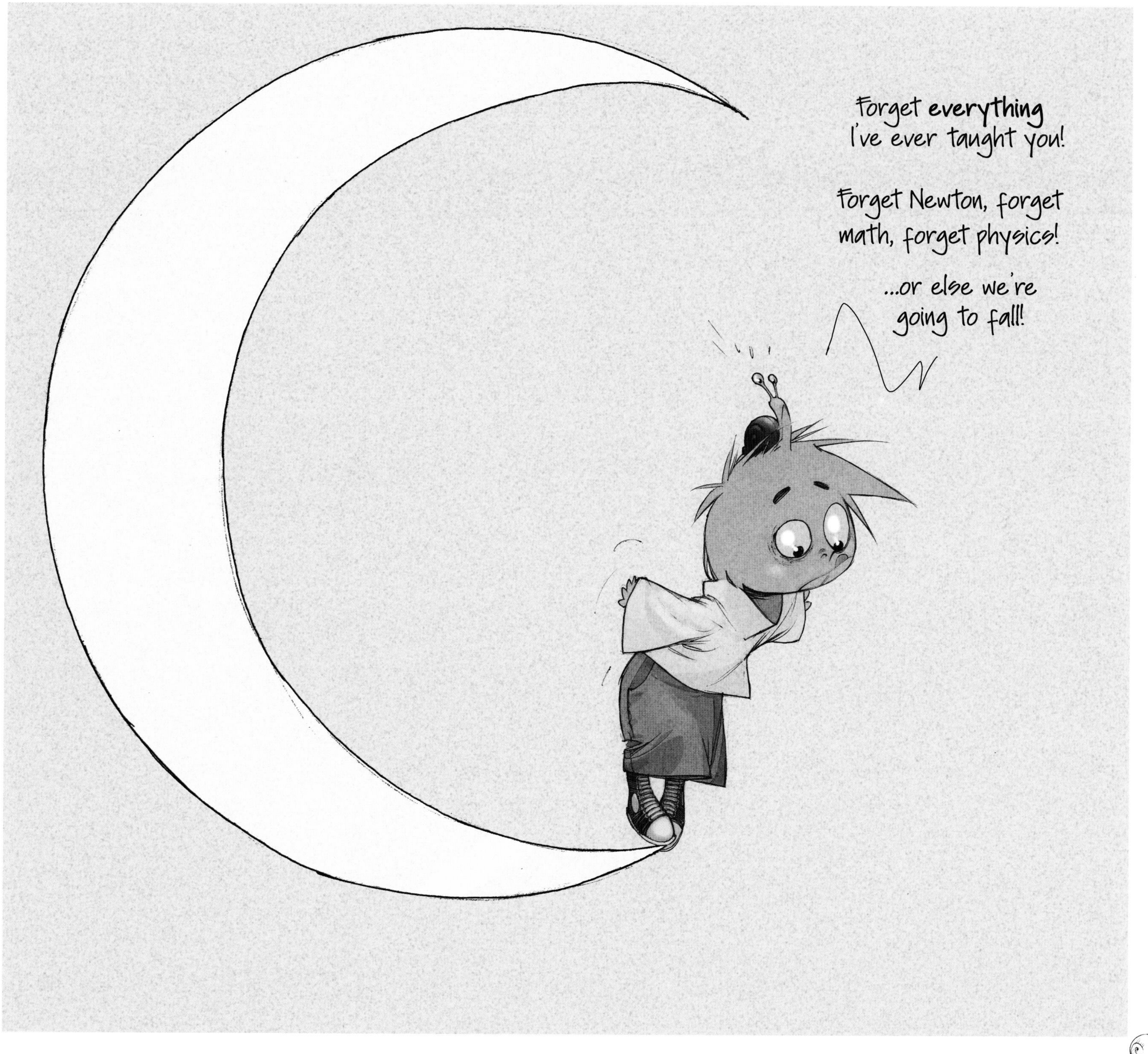
Forget **everything** I've ever taught you!
Forget Newton, forget math, forget physics!
...or else we're going to fall!

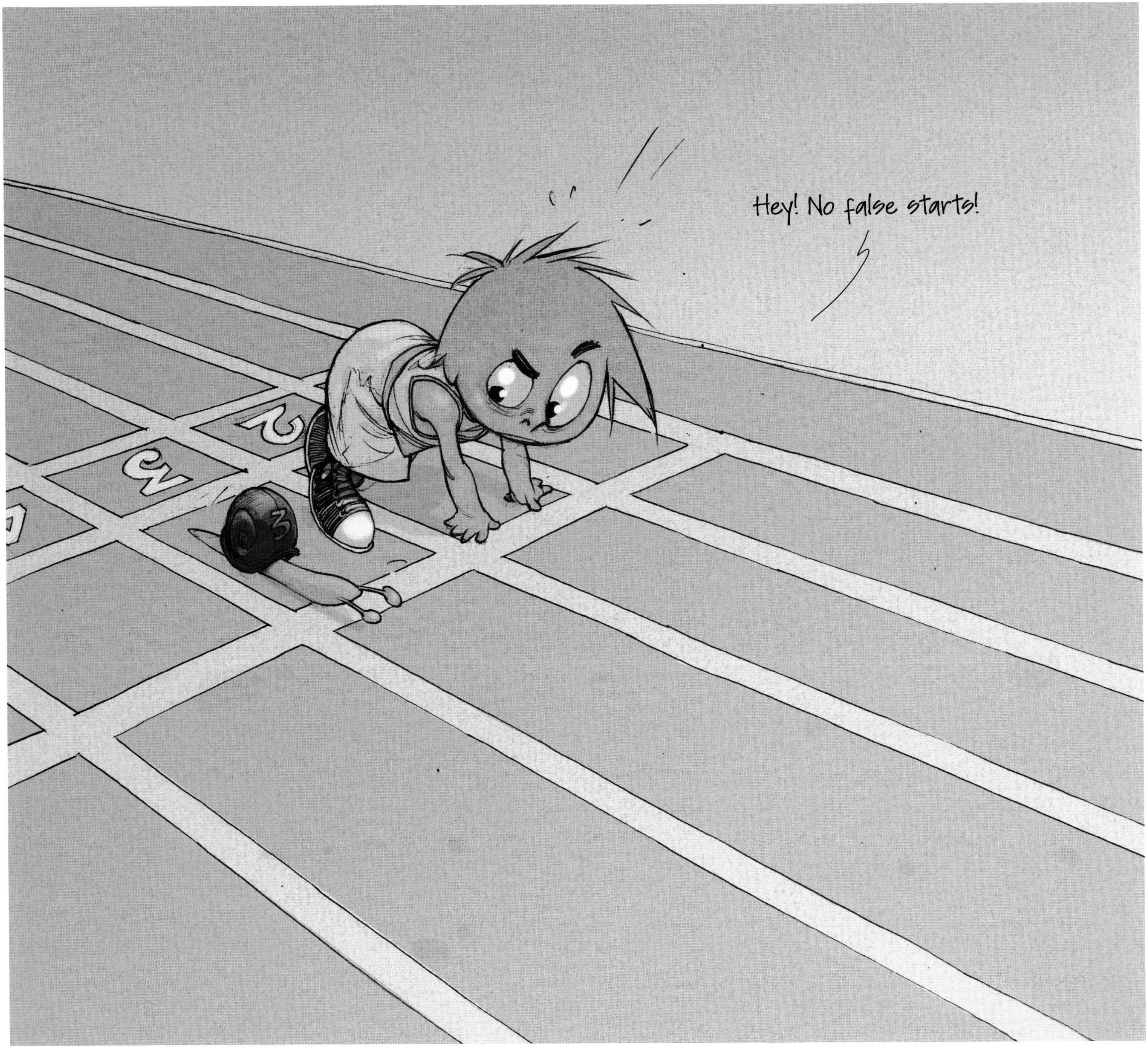
Hey! No false starts!

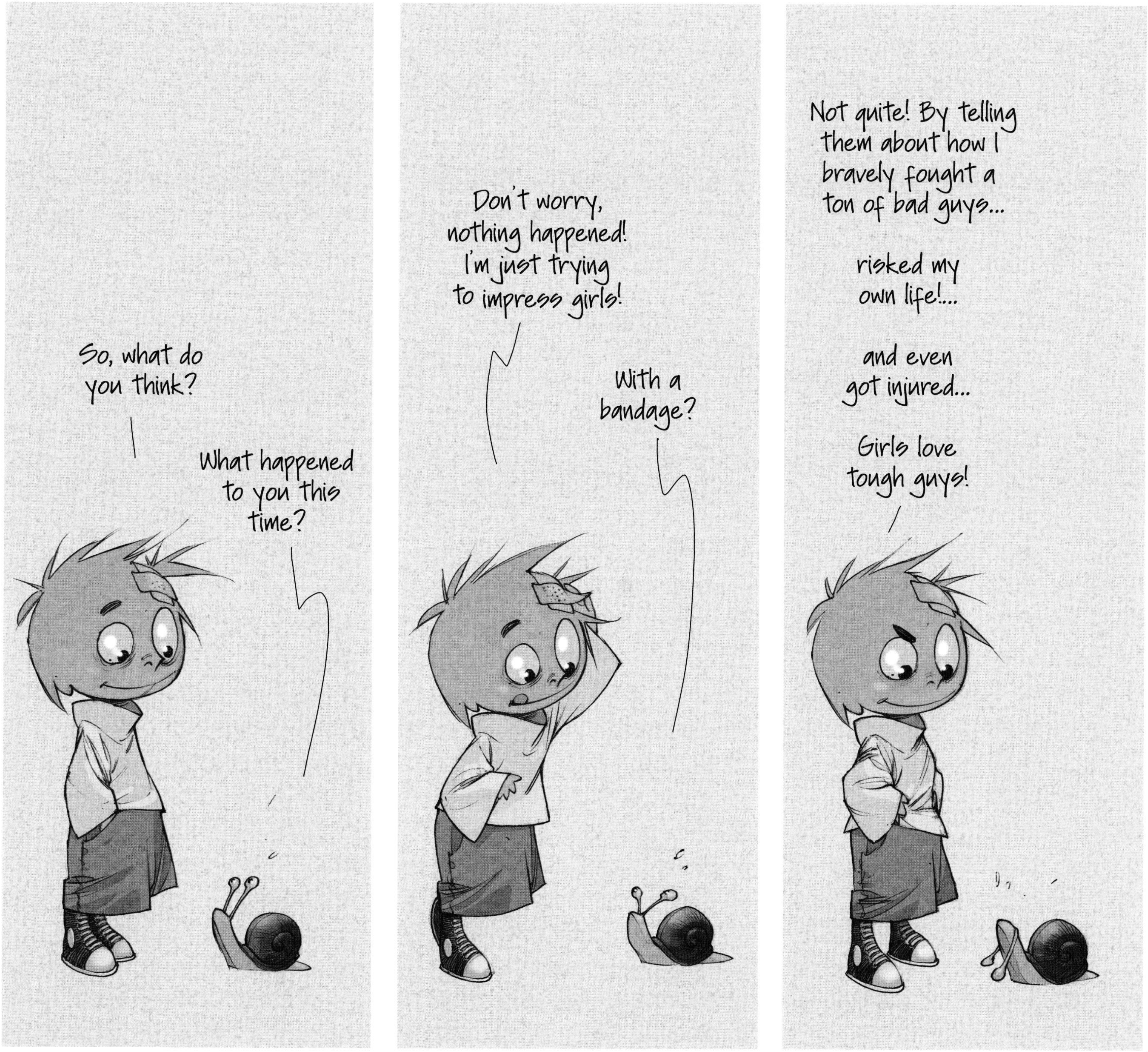
So, what do you think?
What happened to you this time?
Don't worry, nothing happened! I'm just trying to impress girls!
With a bandage?
Not quite! By telling them about how I bravely fought a ton of bad guys...
risked my own life!...
and even got injured...
Girls love tough guys!

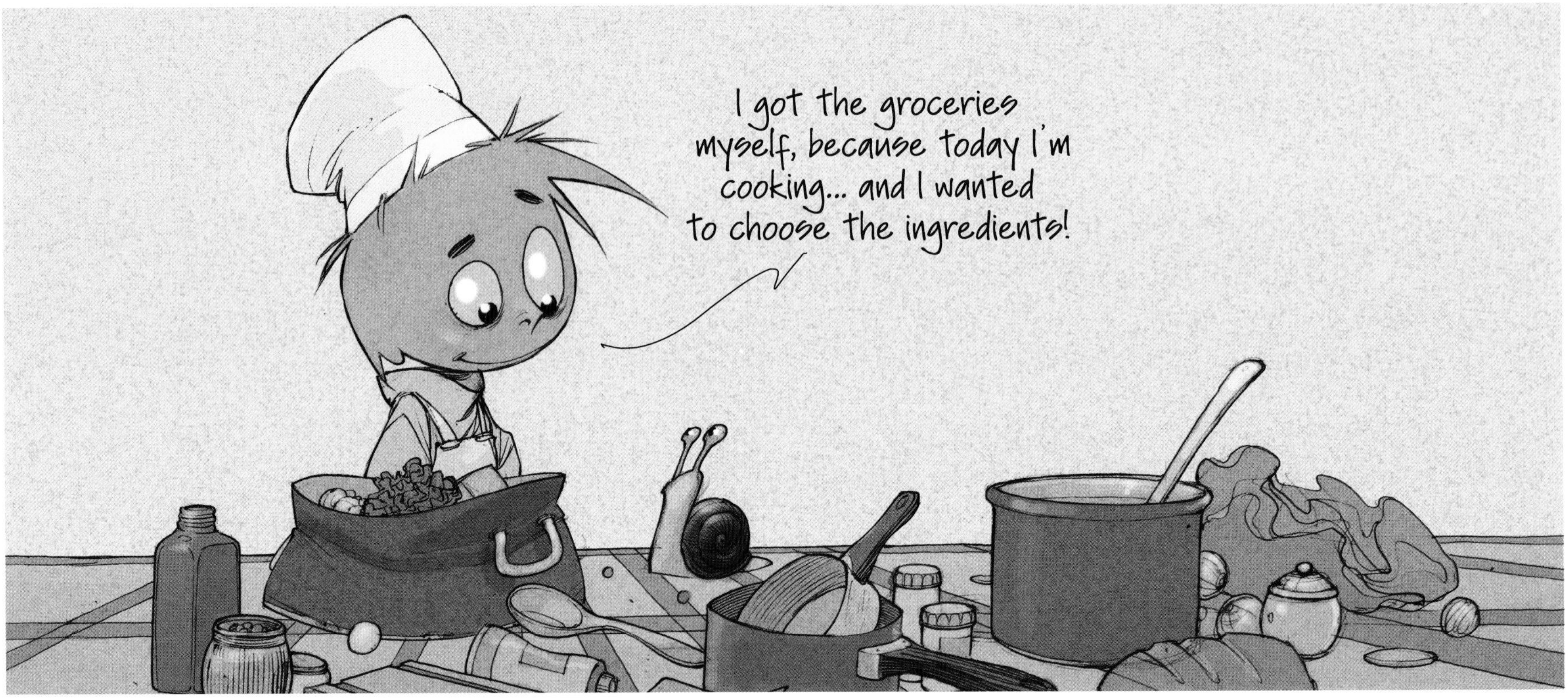
I got the groceries myself, because today I'm cooking... and I wanted to choose the ingredients!

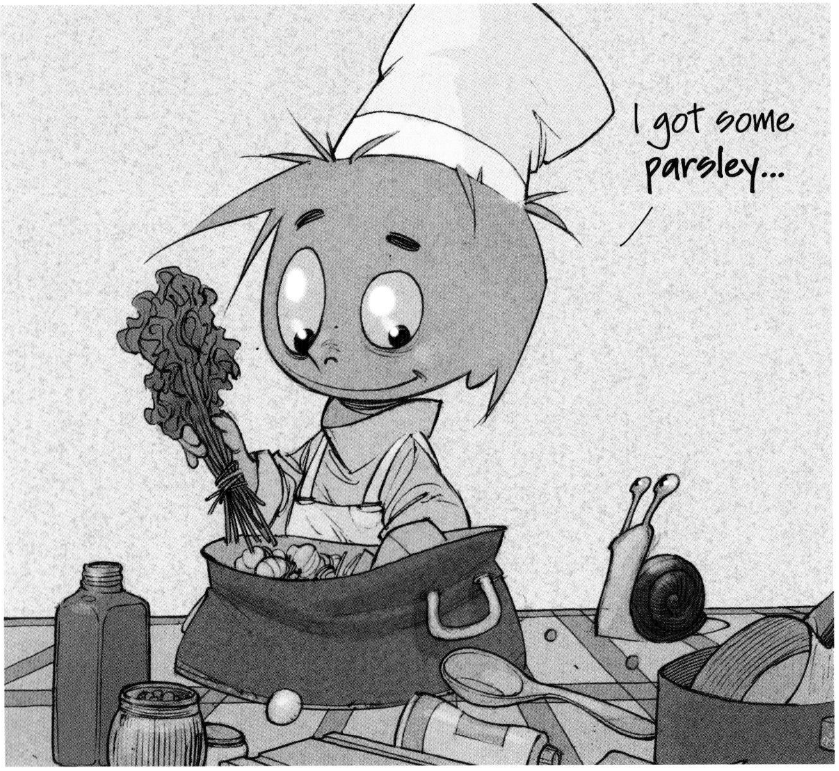
I got some parsley...

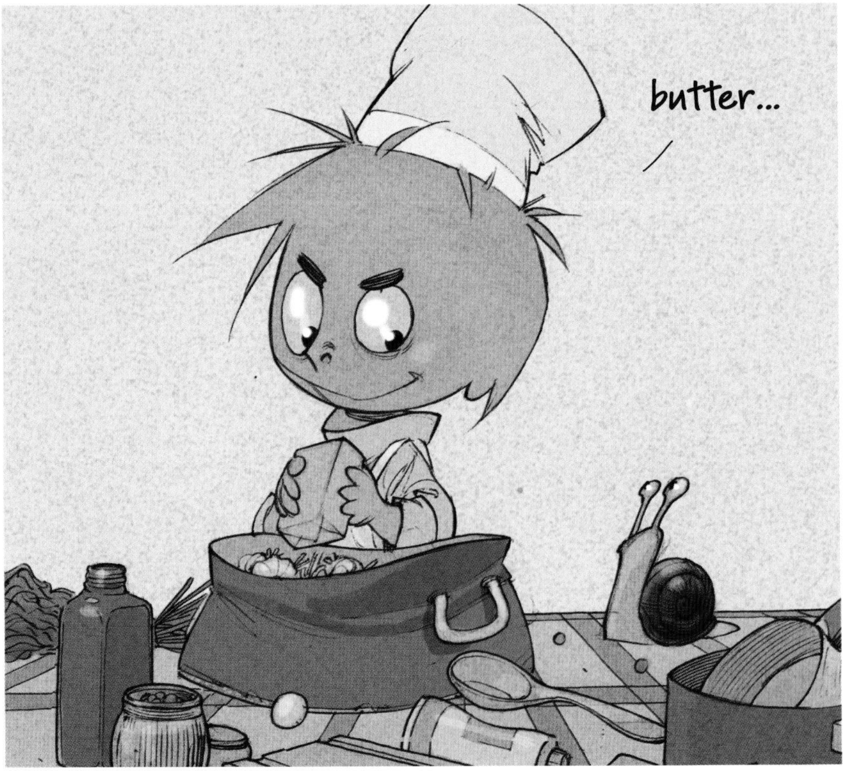
butter...

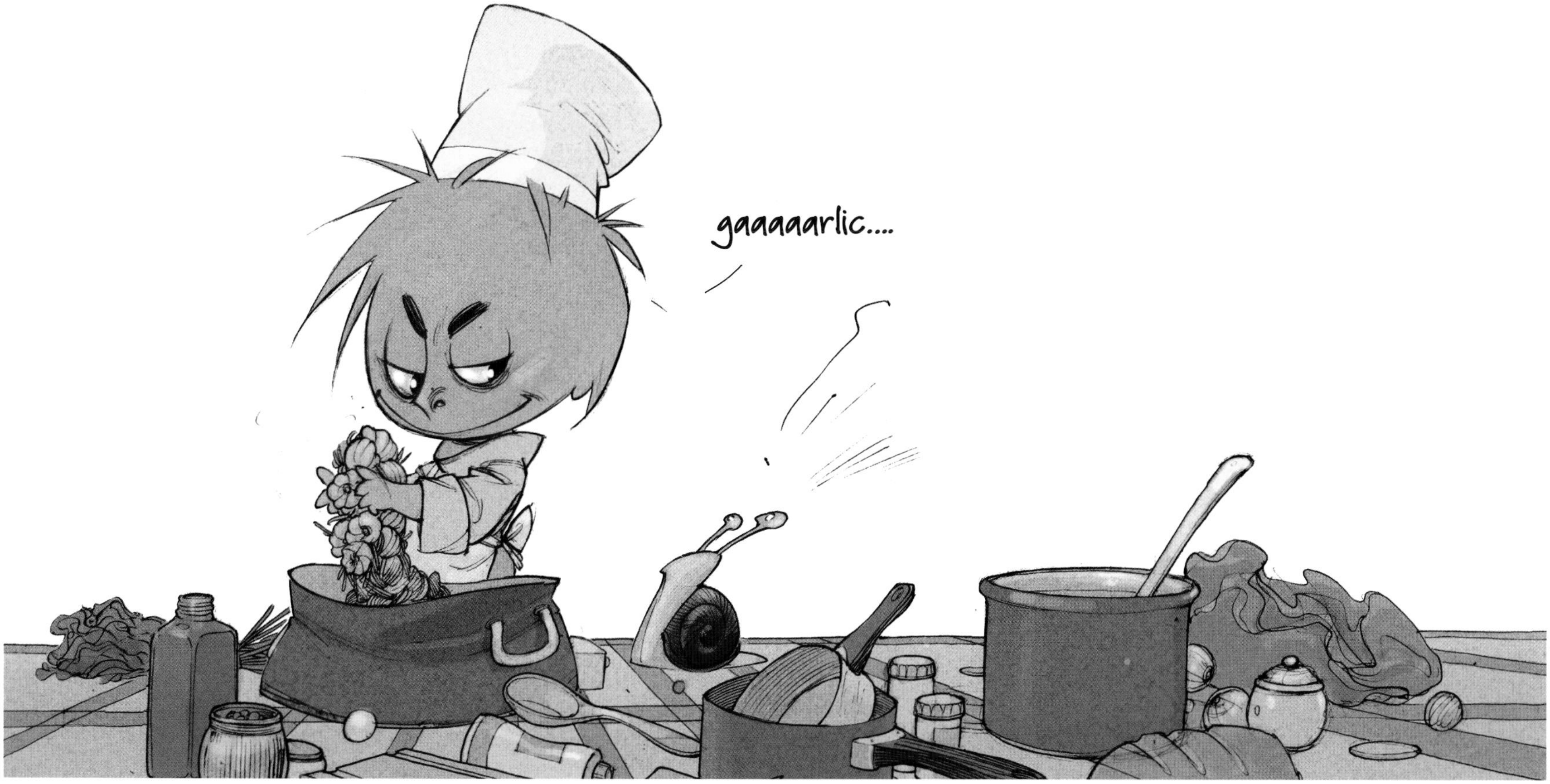
gaaaaarlic....

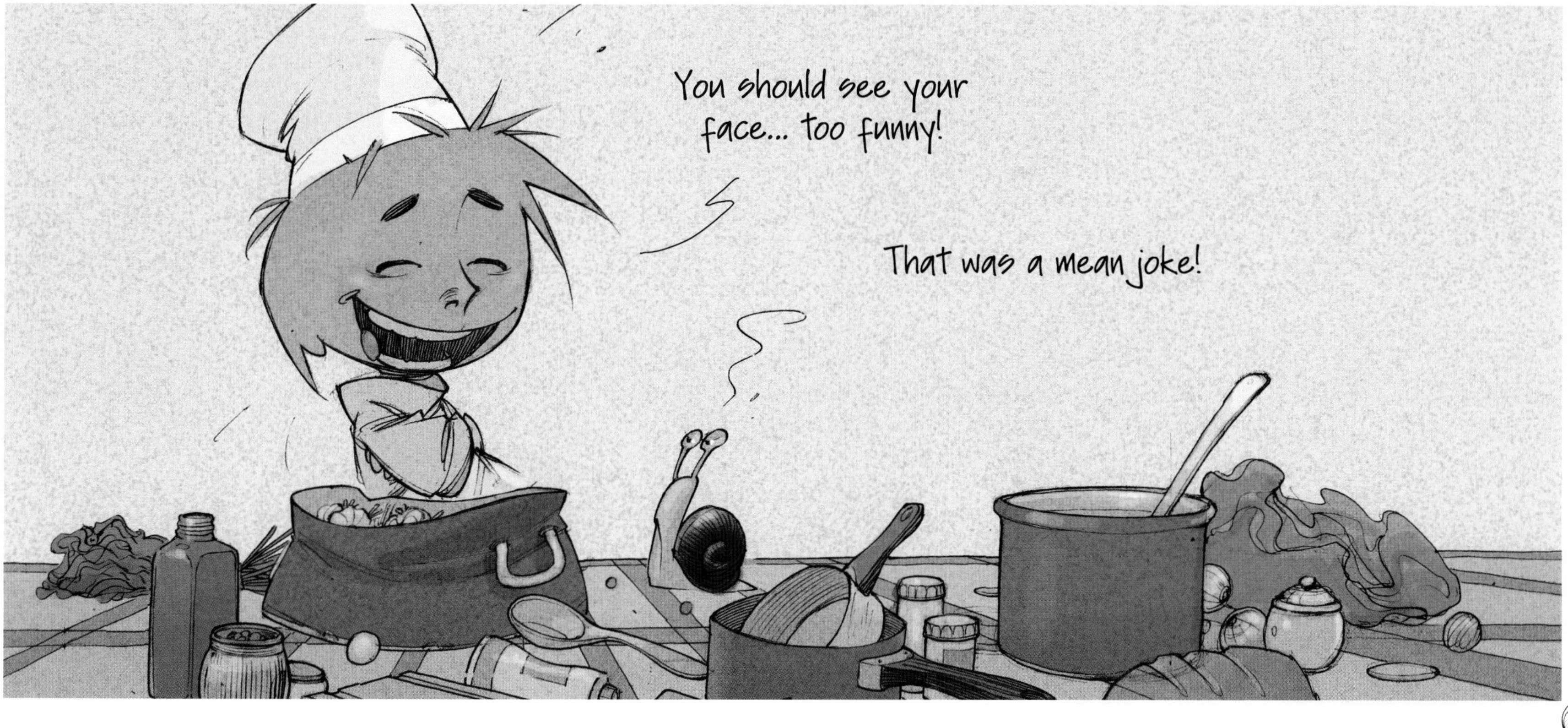
You should see your face... too funny!
That was a mean joke!

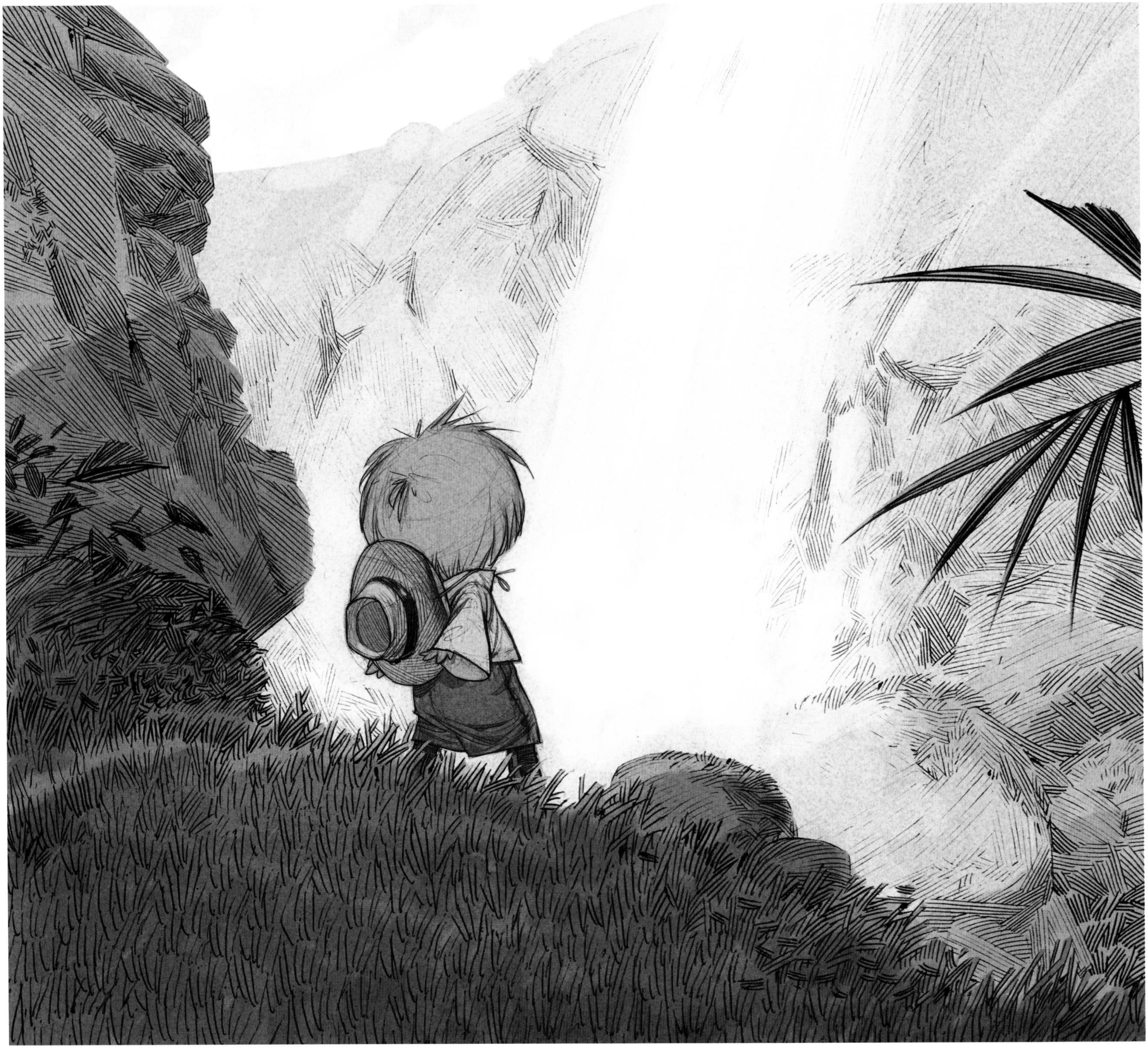

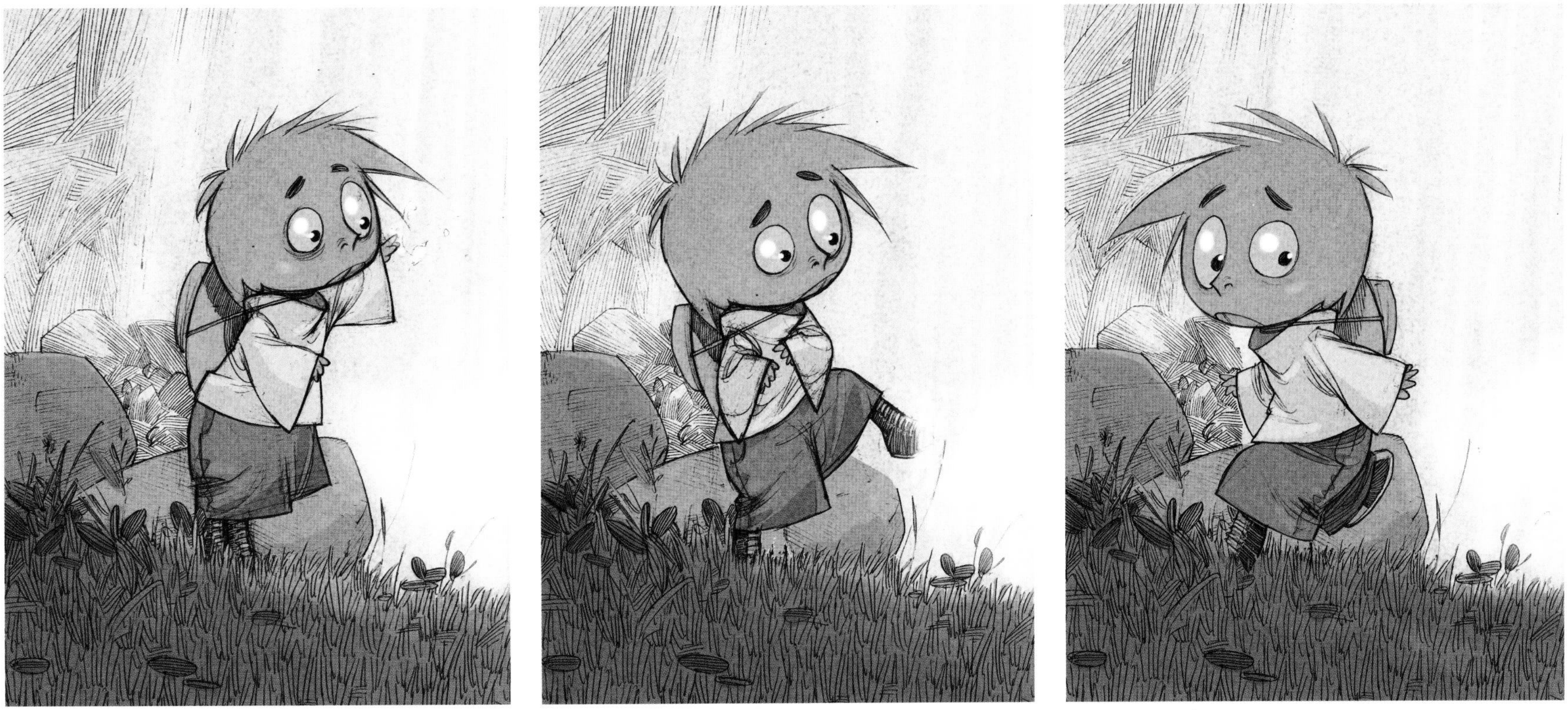

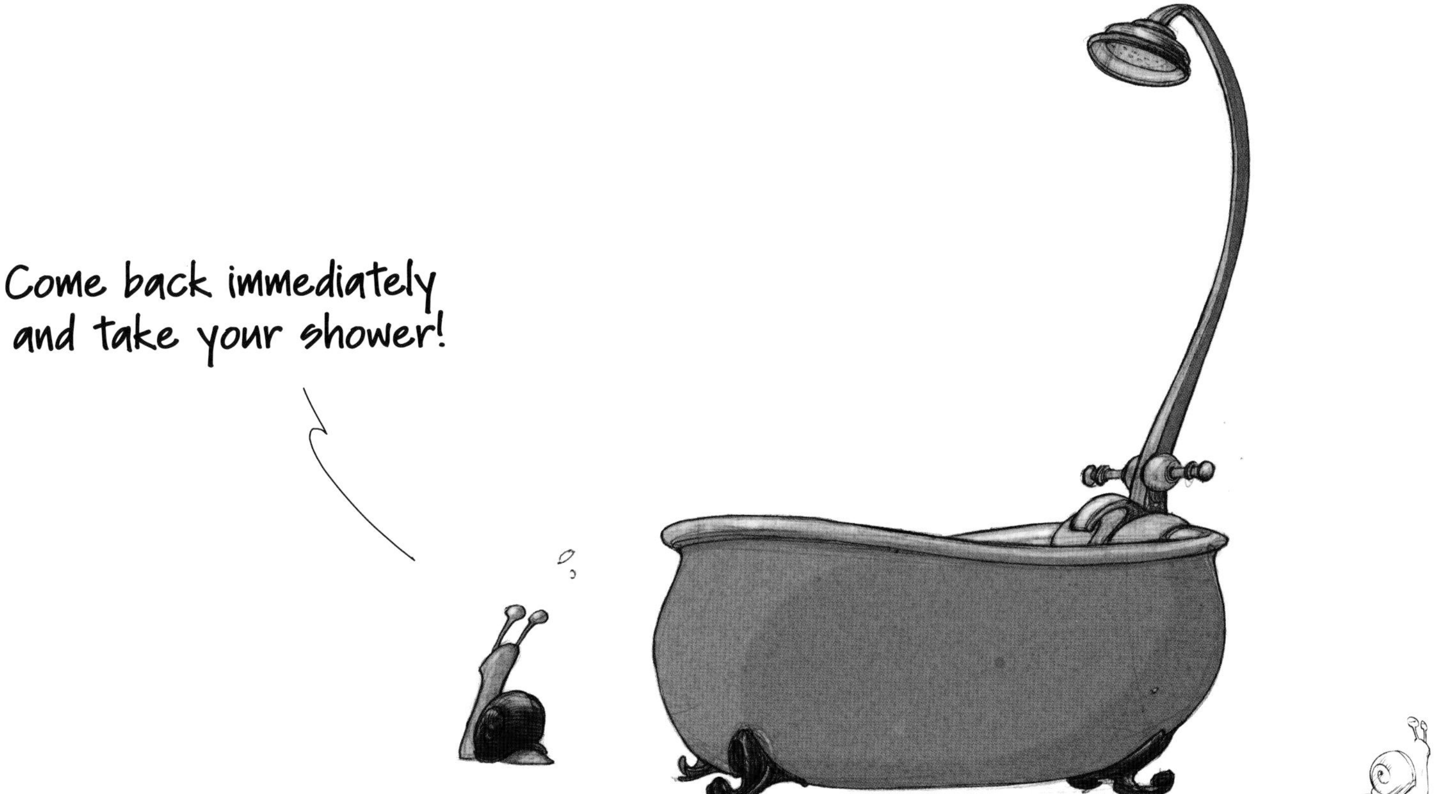
Come back immediately and take your shower!

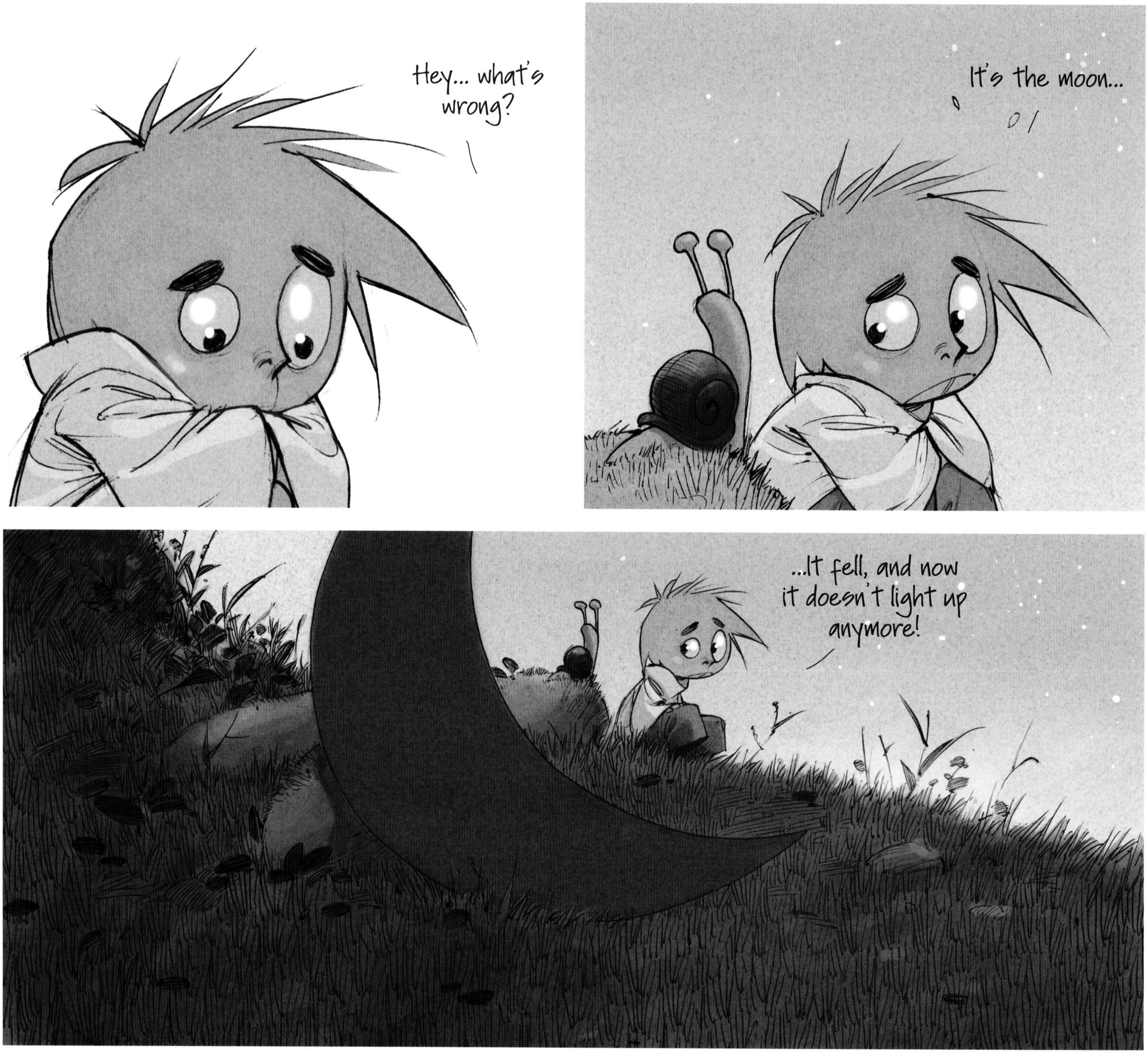
Hey... what's wrong?
It's the moon...
...It fell, and now it doesn't light up anymore!

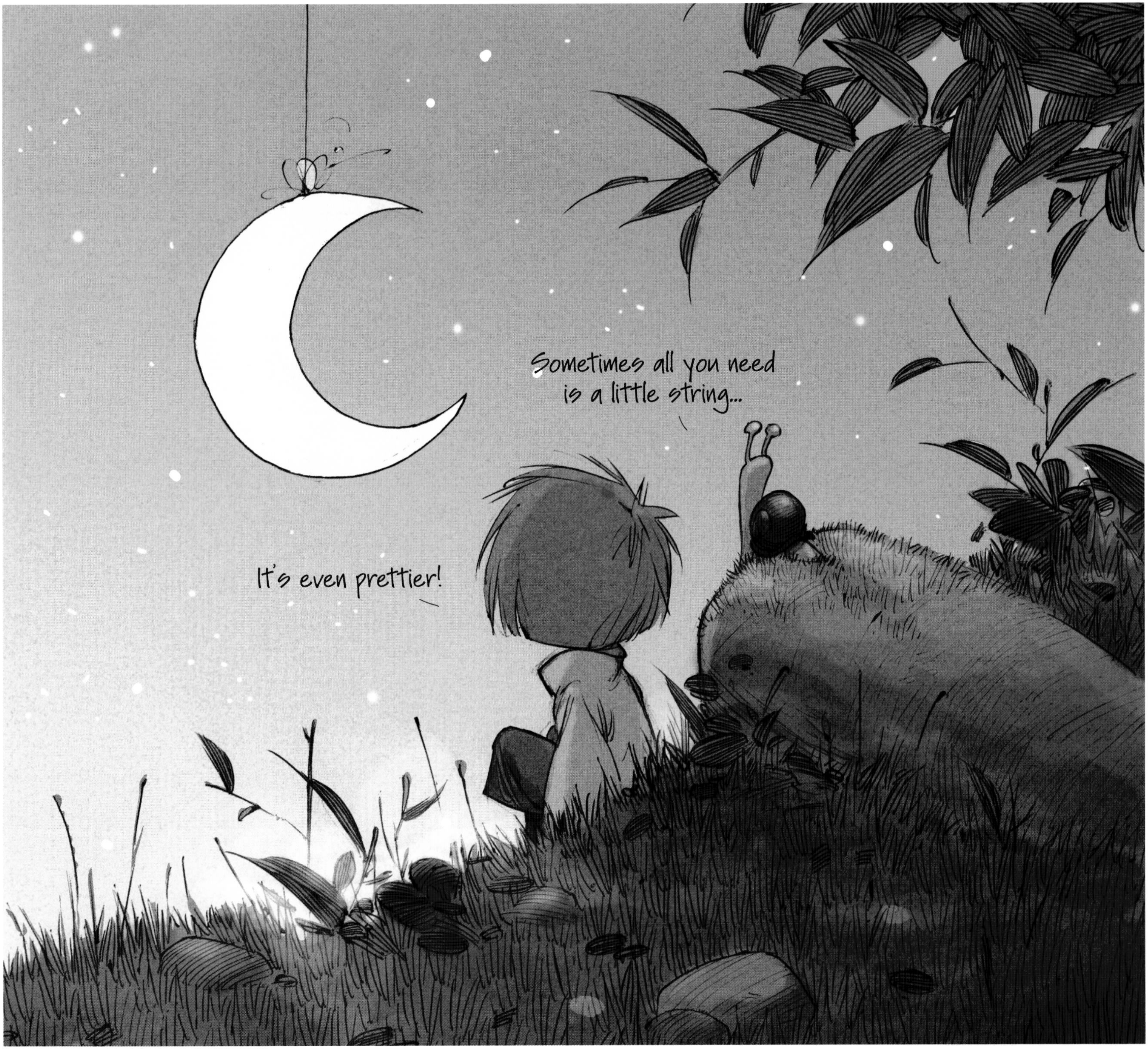
Sometimes all you need
is a little string...
It's even prettier!

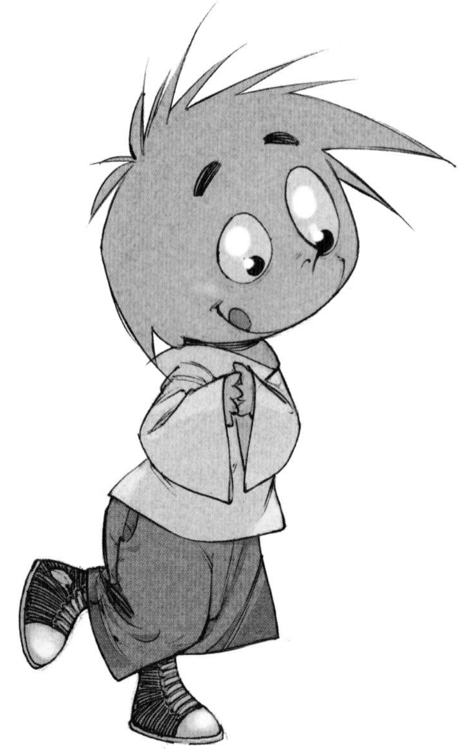
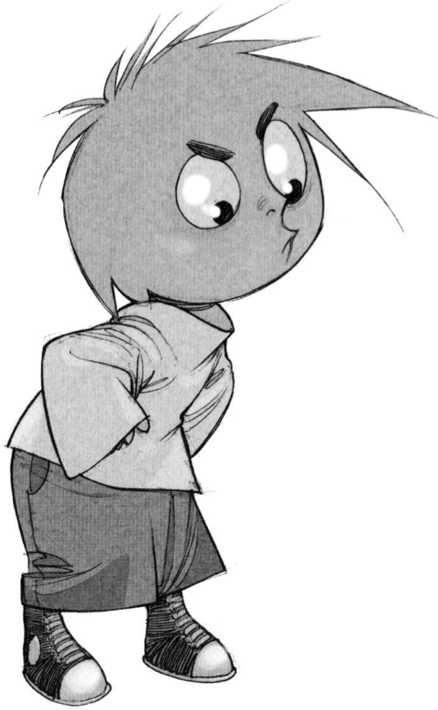
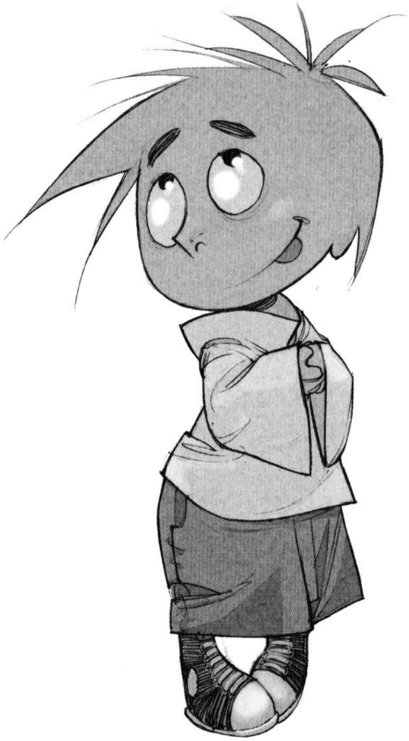
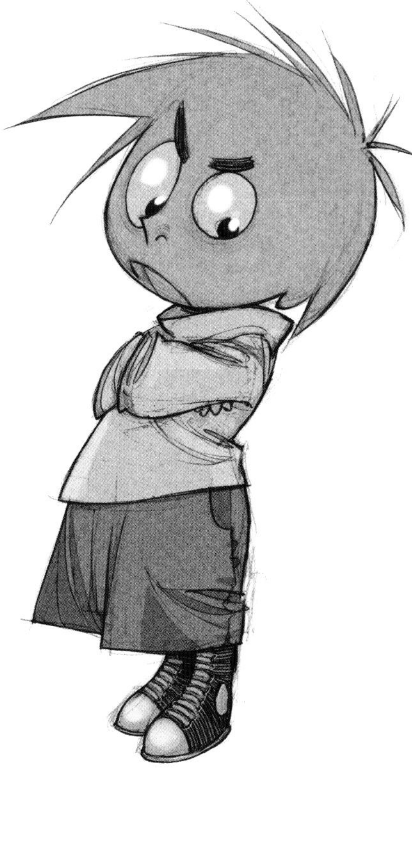

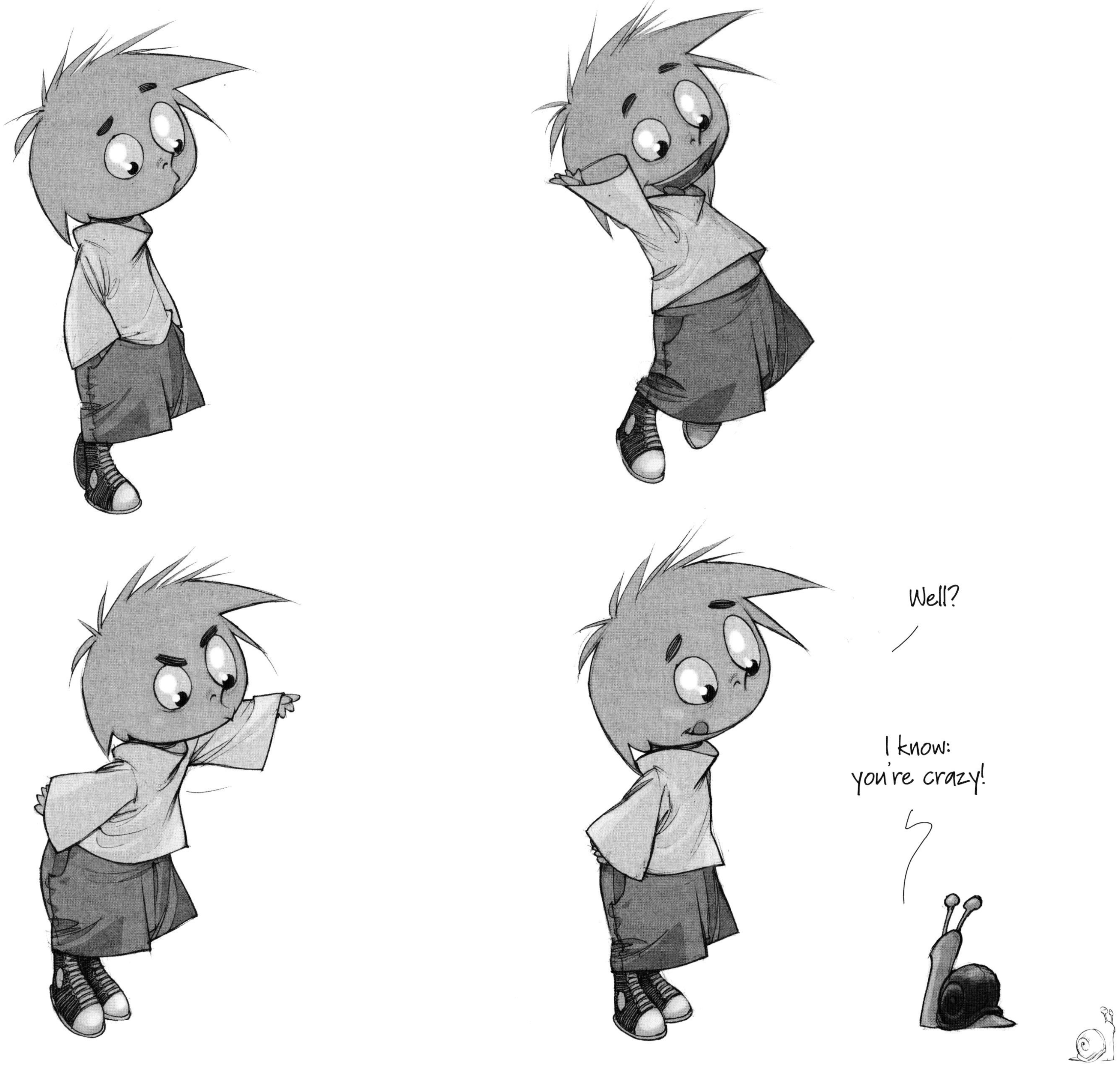
Well?
I know: you're crazy!

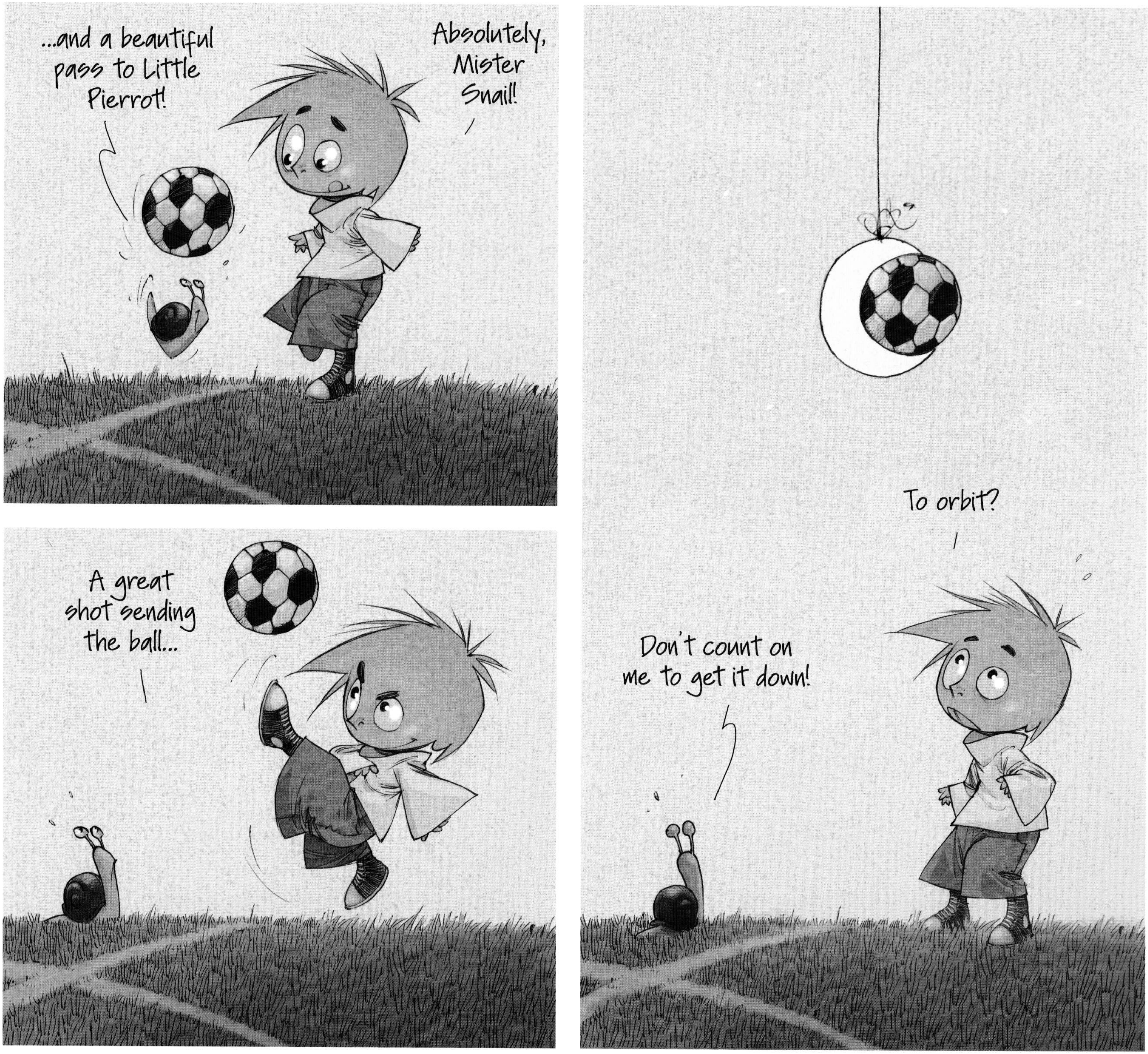
...and a beautiful pass to Little Pierrot!
Absolutely, Mister Snail!
A great shot sending the ball...
To orbit?
Don't count on me to get it down!

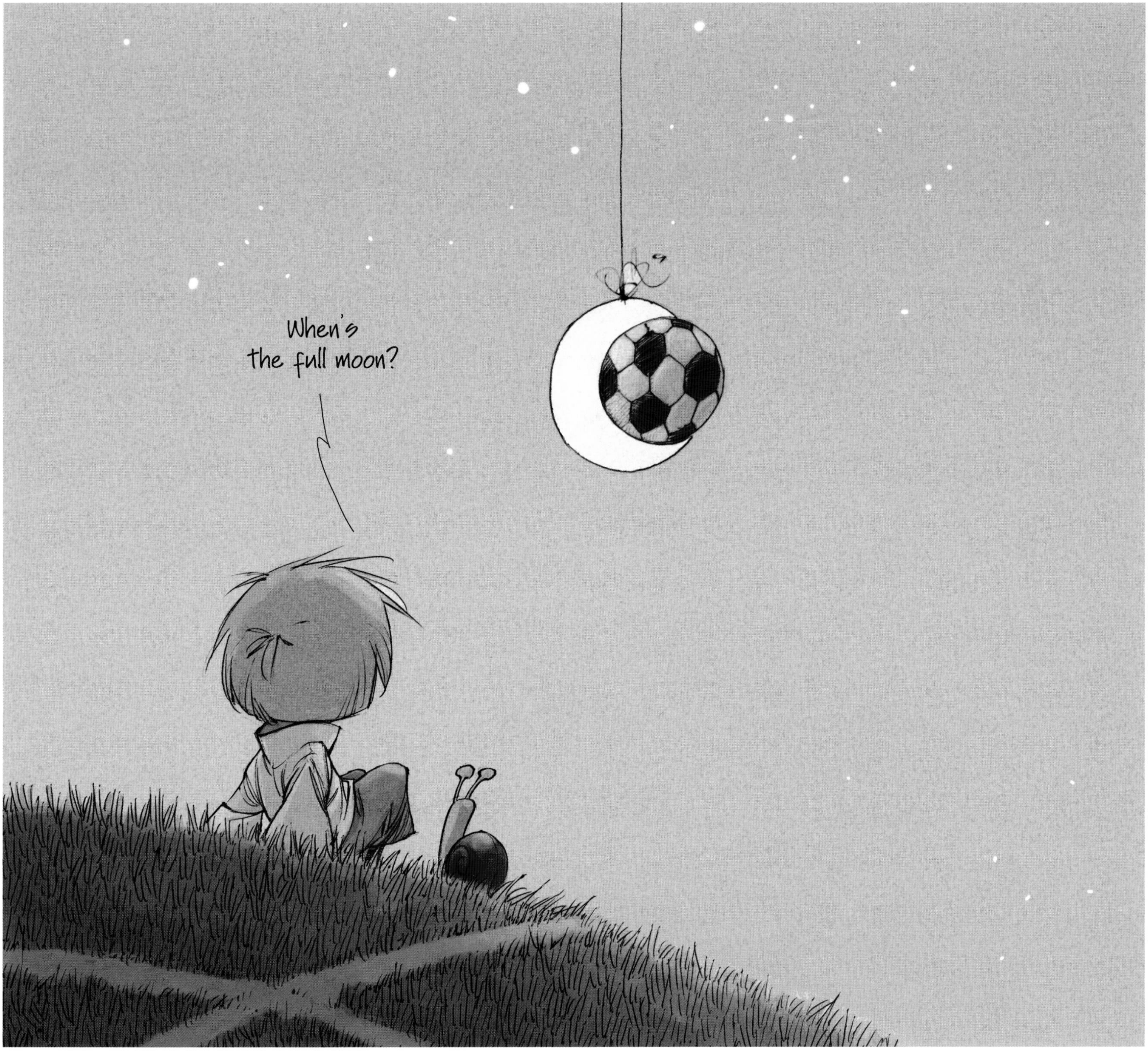
When's
the full moon?

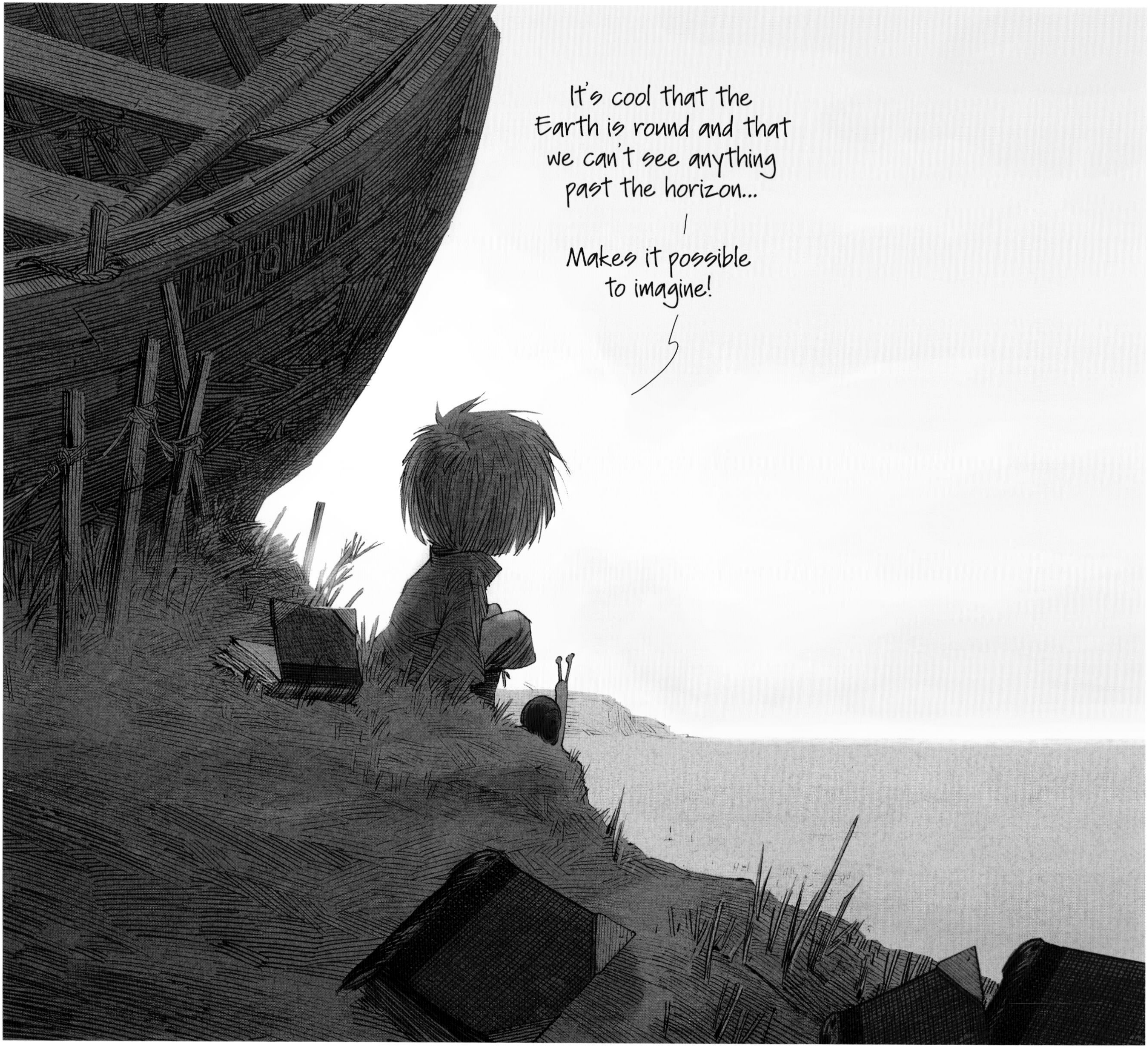
It's cool that the Earth is round and that we can't see anything past the horizon...
Makes it possible to imagine!